Now...a
Harlequin
romance
by Anne Mather
comes to life
on the movie screen

starring
KEIR DULLEA · SUSAN PENHALIGON

Leopard in the Snow

Guest Stars
KENNETH MORE · BILLIE WHITELAW

featuring GORDON THOMSON as MICHAEL
and JEREMY KEMP as BOLT

Produced by JOHN QUESTED and CHRIS HARROP
Screenplay by ANNE MATHER and JILL HYEM
Directed by GERRY O'HARA
An Anglo-Canadian Co-Production

OTHER
Harlequin Romances
by ESSIE SUMMERS

Many of these titles are available at your local bookseller
or through the Harlequin Reader Service.

For a free catalogue listing all available Harlequin Romances,
send your name and address to:

HARLEQUIN READER SERVICE,
M.P.O. Box 707, Niagara Falls, N.Y. 14302
Canadian address: Stratford, Ontario, Canada N5A 6W4

or use order coupon at back of books.

Adair of Starlight Peaks

by

ESSIE SUMMERS

Harlequin Books

TORONTO • LONDON • NEW YORK • AMSTERDAM • SYDNEY

Original hardcover edition published in 1977
by Mills & Boon Limited

ISBN 0-373-02133-X

Harlequin edition published January 1978

PRINTED IN U.S.A.

To Mary Orford
of Melbourne, Australia,
who delights in our mountain ways.

Dreams, books, are each a world; and books, we know, Are a substantial world, both pure and good; Round these, with tendrils strong as flesh and blood, Our pastime and our happiness will grow.

Wordsworth

CHAPTER ONE

JANE GREY carefully packed her oil painting of the Shotover River, knew the customary pang because she was parting with something of her very self, said goodbye to the Canadians who had purchased it, looked at the travellers' cheques they had given her and knew an immense elation, a feeling she'd experienced over and over these last few days. She had done it! She had proved it *was* possible for her mother and herself to make their living in this tourist area.

There was but one snag . . . a formidable one, that of finding somewhere to live. In this artists' paradise that was Queenstown, house prices were high, so were rents, but if by some miracle they could find something reasonable, and live frugally for a year or two, it would pay off.

Mother wanted this so badly that Jane was determined to succeed. Their friends up north had scoffed at the idea, two unknown artists exhibiting their work and daring to think they might earn their daily crust for a family of four! No, no, it was too airy-fairy. They should try for an ordinary job each and rent a flat in some less choice area. They pointed out that Noel, Jane's loved stepfather, had chased rainbows like this all his life and hadn't made much of a go of it. That was precisely why they found themselves in such straitened circumstances now. Fiji was a tourist Mecca too, and he'd only just managed to support them there. Let's face it . . . you had to be in the top class to sell really well. It was obvious that all Mother's well-meaning friends had no confidence in either her or Jane's artistic ability.

They had added that in any case, Queenstown already had its quota of topnotch artists. That was where Jane had rebelled, because she'd seen her mother's gentle blue eyes, so full of courage and hope an hour earlier, mist over, lose their sparkle. Jane had said crisply, 'Well, *they* all had to

7

start. Artists, like authors or musicians, don't have family businesses handed down to them. One has to take the plunge.'

Noel had died in Fiji, on the eve of returning to New Zealand to paint and sell in Central Otago. The previous autumn he and Jane had taken a painting tour of Central, to explore the possibilities. The flaming golds and russets of the mountain and lake scenery had unlocked something in Noel Eastwood that hadn't been apparent before. His Fijian pictures, though attractive, had lacked something.

Jane had been surprised that Noel had been able to buy the motorised caravan they'd hired at first for their two-month stay. He'd left it in Christchurch, to pick it up when they came to New Zealand permanently. They'd thought at first, when they reached their Fijian home, that he was just tired after the trip. He reluctantly agreed to see his doctor, but died from a stroke before the appointment could take place. Even now, thinking about it, Jane knew a twist of pain at her heart. She was sure that, at last, he would have found his métier here beside Lake Wakatipu.

And she would have found hers. This was the type of country she wanted to paint, rugged, with a grandeur that challenged the inward eye and the brush of the artist to re-produce . . . the incredible colours of lakes and rivers, the sculpted gorges and the trees that clothed them in such beauty, gentling the landscapes into a harmony of trunk and bough and leaf; the glinting snow-pockets, the tender lights of sunrises, the flaming palette of the sunsets.

They found Noel had mortgaged his insurance to buy the caravan. Nothing underhand about it, merely a desire to save Mother worry. It hadn't been a very adequate insurance at that, in view of today's prices, and their house in Fiji had still carried a substantial mortgage. The balance merely pro-vided them with a modest sum against emergencies.

Mother had said, looking at the landscapes Jane had produced when travelling with Noel, 'These are better than anything you've ever done. You have my grandfather's undoubted gift. I wish, oh, how I wish, you'd had the chance to live in Central and establish yourself there.' That was when the idea had been born ... they would try it, even without Noel.

They'd come first to Auckland friends, dear folk, but so set in their ways that they'd been horrified at the risk of attempting this. At first they would have Noel's stock of Central Otago landscapes to sell, it was true, but after that, there would be just Jane's and her mother's. These latter were watercolours, executed with a delicacy of touch akin to Chinese drawings, and held something, Jane knew, of the nostalgia her mother had always known for New Zealand. They hadn't sold well in Fiji, naturally, for they were almost all of Canterbury, therefore not good buying for the tourists who came to Fiji and wanted the bolder splashes of the tropical splendour of their holiday venue.

Jane had whisked her mother away from the Cassandra-like croakings of her well-meaning friends, and while staying in Oamaru had found a very reasonable flat where she could leave her mother with Lauris and Louise, the eleven-year-old twins, while she tried out the selling possibilities of the tourist area.

She had found a small shop temporarily empty, in the Queenstown Mall, in which to exhibit her wares; first Noel's and her mother's, then, when Noel's had sold out, her own. It had been their mutual interest in painting that had drawn Noel and her young widowed mother together first, in the art circles of Christchurch. Jane had been quite young. She couldn't remember her own father, only a harsh grandfather of whom she'd stood in awe. How that grandfather had mocked at the pictures his widowed daughter-in-law had attempted. Yet now they were going to help provide their bread-and-butter.

They had sold surprisingly well here, hundreds of miles south of Christchurch. Some to tourists who'd been there; some to residents who knew and loved Canterbury too; some for their sheer beauty. Mother had captured its elusive charm so well, the curves of the bridges that spanned the rippling Avon, the tracery of delicate willow-leaves weeping down into the waters, the wading birds of the estuary, ducks winging out to sea in black silhouette and winged grace, over seas stained with sunset colours . . .

Now these walls were almost empty, but there was a case packed with scenes of Lake Wanaka and Lake Hawea, her next port of call. Jane's eyes roved over the remaining pictures. Time to move on. Her canvases were all signed with her second name, Esmeralda Grey, because Jane was too similar to her mother's signature. Mother was June, and when she'd first started painting, naturally her name had still been Grey. So Jane had become Esmeralda. As a child she'd been rather sensitive about her old-fashioned second name. Perhaps because the harsh grandfather had chosen it for her, though no one knew why. Mother and her own father, his son, had wisely put Jane in front of it.

She wondered if it was worth while keeping the shop open any longer. In came a little woman who'd been in before, who had lingered quite a time before that small picture she'd painted down-lake, of a weeping willow leaning over the sapphire waters with the steep, unroaded mountains of the hinterland rising in the background.

Now she gave a quick glance at Jane, hesitated, then went over to the picture and stood before it, gazing with an intensity that was noticeable. There was longing in it, a pathetic, almost hungry look. It disturbed Jane. It was reminiscent of the way she and Mother had felt in Auckland as they gazed at lovely homes far beyond their means. Jane had priced her pictures high. They were worth it, and they needed the money, but . . .

She went across, said, 'Hullo, sorry I've not many left. Not so much to choose from now.'

The shabby little figure turned. Goodness, age hadn't faded these eyes. They were as blue as the lake. She had a broad brow beneath hair that had been gold once, and an air of serenity oddly at variance with that wistful, longing look.

The little woman smiled, 'Oh, lack of choice wouldn't matter to me. If I was buying, this would be the one I'd want. I've loved that tree ever since I went to live down-lake, and it's gone.'

'Gone? I painted it just last autumn.'

'It was blown into the lake in a freak storm in July. It looked so pathetic lying half-submerged in the water that a dear young friend of mine had it dragged away and he planted another, just a sapling. But I miss every curve of that tree.'

Jane didn't hesitate. 'I've had a much more successful exhibition than I'd dreamed I'd have. Most of my pictures have gone overseas, with the tourists. I'd love to think one found its home here, with someone who had loved that tree in its full pride, when it gave shade to picnickers when the sun was too hot, and shelter to countless birds. I know people are embarrassed when offered something from someone they're not acquainted with, but would you give me the very real pleasure of giving you this? Even if I am a total stranger!'

Colour, carnation-bright, flowed up into the lined cheeks and the sapphire eyes lit up. Her voice was quite charming, husky, low, even a little tremulous. 'But you see, dear, you're *not* a total stranger. Your kind thought has given me the courage to say what I came in to say ... my name is Esmeralda Grey too, and I'm your step-grandmama!'

Jane got such a shock that she instinctively took a step backwards.

The other Esmeralda Grey said gently, 'I've taken your breath away, as well I might. But you were named for me. Long ago I broke my engagement to your grandfather, then in the last year of his life, when he was old and lonely and, as I found, more crabbed than ever, I married him. I loved the picture, yes, but the real reason I came back was because there'd not be so many people about and I might find the spunk to make myself known.'

Jane said, 'I'll shut the shop. I can sell the rest in Wanaka.' She turned the key, said, 'Come on into the back and we'll have a cup of tea together.' She noticed that the small crêpey hands were trembling.

There was something very gracious about this little lady. She had put that criticism of Henry Grey in her explanation, Jane was sure, so that she wouldn't put her namesake on the defensive. Otherwise Jane would have had to explain that her grandfather and her mother—his daughter-in-law—had been estranged, so that she hadn't known of his second marriage.

Esmeralda chattered more lightly as the kettle boiled. 'I peered at the signature on the paintings in the window and such a shock to see my own unusual name. I'd thought it was just your middle name. That you were Jane.'

'I am. I use the Esmeralda only because Mother exhibits as June Grey and it's too confusing—though Mother's always known as Willy because she was June Willymore before she married my father. So I settled on Esmeralda. I like it.'

The older Esmeralda said, 'It suits you ... with your lovely goldy-brown hair and green eyes and that green artist's smock, it's just perfect. Oh, this tea is good. I needed that. I lingered a long time earlier, because I thought I could tell by your voice if you'd be kind about the relationship or not. Then when you made that kindest of offers, that clinched it. Now you'll want to know how I came to marry Henry.'

'Yes. We didn't know till a year or more after he died that he'd gone. There was no one to tell us, we'd moved round so much. He'd cast Mother off long since, in Christchurch, because she married again. She'd managed as a young widow for so long, working at a not very congenial job so that she could be home when I got in from school, and managing to do most of the work in Grandfather's home as well as ours. That started the trouble. She refused to move in with him, knowing it would be no sort of life for a child. But she looked after him so well. When she married Noel he'd have nothing more to do with either of us.

'It worried Mother for years because even if he wasn't a kindred spirit, she wanted to keep in touch with him for my own father's sake. But he just shut the door in her face or banged the phone up in her ear every time she tried to contact him. You can do nothing with such people.'

Esmeralda nodded. 'He was so domineering, so selfish. I'd been completely fascinated with him at twenty; he was so handsome. But I soon realised that what I'd taken for a masterful man was really just a bossy one. I saw the writing on the wall. He was not a man to live a lifetime with. But I dealt his pride a great blow. He turned very cynical. Your own grandmother, his first wife, was a gentle little thing, very sweet, a school friend of us both. She'd always loved him and had she lived longer would have gentled him, I'm sure. Henry became most possessive about his son and in turn, when Gerald died, he became possessive about your mother.'

'Yet you finally married him. Why?'

Esmeralda's smile was winsome and philosophical. 'It eased my conscience. I felt I'd turned him into a bitter man, and I'd had such a happy life. I'd married a man with a really sunny nature, the sort of man who never took one for granted, who knew that marriage vows weren't just for faithfulness and for sharing one's worldly goods, but also for cherishing. We had thirty-five very happy years together and retired in Queenstown itself. We had a lovely home with a view over the lake. Our one regret was that we had no family.

'Thomas had been gone ten years when on a visit to Christchurch I ran into Henry. He looked so sad, lonely and shabby. Of course it was his own fault. I even thought, foolishly, that I might bring about a reconciliation between your mother and him. I talked to him of his only grandchild, but I'd not realised that the bitterness in him was granite-hard.

'Then I found he was heavily in debt. It meant—well, it reduced our circumstances, but no matter. I was able to nurse him to the end. When he became completely dependent upon me I saw in him again something of the Henry I'd loved in my green and salad days. I couldn't find any trace of you among his papers. All he ever told me was that he'd asked his son to call you Esmeralda. I liked that. But to have found you is like a dream come true. Would you and your mother come and stay with me down-lake for a holiday?' she went on. 'Or does your mother not want any reminders of what must have been the unhappiest time of her life?'

'I'm sure Mother would love it,' said Jane, 'but there's a chance we may come here to live. I have twin half-sisters, Louise and Lauris, both eleven. My stepfather died a few months ago and we resolved to carry out what he'd been planning—and that was to settle here, paint our pictures, sell them. But Queenstown is too expensive for us, so I'm off to Wanaka tomorrow to look round there. That's a good tourist area too. I've an idea I might find a farm cottage to rent, and get a souvenir shop to display my pictures and Mother's on a commission basis. We wouldn't be far from you and I'm sure Mother would love to meet you.' Jane looked reflective. 'Even Noel, my stepfather, was mighty short on relations. You're next door to one. Seeing I was named for you, may I call you godmother? I've always thought I'd love to have a godmother. It's such a lovely affectionate sort of word.'

Again that flush of pleasure stained Esmeralda's cheeks. 'It would delight my sentimental old heart!'

They chatted on, each conscious of happiness. Esmeralda said, 'Oh, I do wish you weren't going on to Wanaka tomorrow. Why didn't I discover you earlier? I'd have loved you to stay with me.'

'That would have been lovely, though I've been most comfortable in the camping-ground with my caravan.' A thought struck Jane. 'Godmother . . . how about coming with me to Wanaka? I'm putting in five days there. You could stay with me in the caravan. It's roomy. We could get to know each other that way, and you could help me hunt for a cottage. How about it? Would you like that?'

Would Esmeralda like that? She was starry-eyed at the prospect. 'Child, I'd adore it. Rory would look after my chooks for me. And the cats.'

'Rory?'

'He's got the homestead behind me. He'll bring me to meet you tomorrow morning. What time will you be leaving? Oh, and talking of time, I've promised to meet him at five at the grocer's. We're both picking up provisions. I must run. I'll bring him back and we'll finalise the time.' She darted off, all eagerness.

Jane knew a lightness of heart not hers for some time. They would not come as strangers here. Esmeralda was almost family.

The door opened and Esmeralda was dwarfed by the man who came in behind her, tall, broad, dark . . . no, not quite dark, chestnut-haired. His face was aquiline, all planes and angles, and he had grooved cheeks which gave him a slightly forbidding look. Silly thing to think! Fair men had a head start on other men, they looked sunny-natured.

Esmeralda drew him forward. 'Jane Esmeralda, this is Rory Adair of Starlight, my good neighbour and dear friend.'

Jane said hullo and added. 'That sounds like a name in a Border ballad; how lovely to be Adair of Starlight. I'm sure Walter Scott could have made something of that.'

Before he could answer her, Esmeralda said, 'It's Starlight Peaks really, way down past the Remarkables, the most beautiful place in the world.'

Rory Adair said, 'It's always shortened to Starlight. Makes a sort of trio. You've probably heard of Moonlight in behind Queenstown, where you can go riding—and there's a sheep-station called Fairlight, beyond Kingston at the foot of the lake, and us. We're between Garston and Athol, further south.'

Jane said pleasantly, 'What delightful names. And Rory, I suppose, is short for Roderick?'

'Almost. My father's called that. Without a "k", which doesn't, of course, matter. He gets Rod for short. I'm Broderic, son of Roderic, and get Rory—from intimates.'

Jane had the distinct impression she was being set off at a distance. Oh, how absurd of her!

Before she could say anything more he said, 'Mrs Grey tells me you are Henry Grey's granddaughter.'

Jane had no idea how much of the family history and its estrangements he'd know, so she just nodded and said lightly, 'Yes, quite a coincidence that my step-grandmama should notice the name I use for my paintings and come in. Had I used Jane Grey she'd probably have passed me by.'

Suddenly his face looked sterner and more craggy, if that were possible. 'And on the strength of this newly-discovered relationship, you're taking Esmeralda to Wanaka with you?'

Jane felt herself tauten. 'I think we'll both enjoy it. I just suggested it because I must leave here tomorrow. I assure you, Mr Adair, I'll take great care of her. I'm a very careful driver.'

He considered that, then, 'You know, of course, that caravans are not allowed over the Crown Range?'

Her voice was crisp. 'I do. Mine is a motorised caravan, though, which might make a difference, seeing it doesn't involve towing; but in any case I'd want to go through the Kawarau Gorge again. I love it. And if you go to Wanaka from this side, you have your back to the views. My stepfather and I came from Wanaka to here. He was with me last autumn.' Her voice trembled a little. She turned hastily to the counter, picked up Esmeralda's willow picture which she'd already wrapped, and handed it to her.

Broderic Adair said, 'I'll bring her to Frankton to meet you.'

16

Jane's voice was cool. 'Perhaps that'll be inconvenient for you—it would be no trouble for me to come down-lake to collect my godmother.'

His voice too was crisp and cool. 'Oh, it's no trouble. After all, Esmeralda is regarded as one of the Adair family.'

'Then if you name a time I'll undertake to be at the Frankton Arm Junction to take her on board.'

'Better for me to bring her here, rather than wait about there.'

Jane felt nettled. 'Just make a time, I'll be there. Because punctuality is one of my few virtues.'

'It would have to be too early. I've a stock agent coming to see me at nine.'

Jane said sweetly, 'Then make it seven-thirty at the Junction. That will allow time for any hold-up you might have on the way home. Myself, I'm a great believer in allowing for the unforeseen.'

Broderic Adair said, 'Sounds pessimistic for someone your age, Miss Grey. More like Mrs Bindle.'

'Mrs Bindle? Who is she?'

'A character in a series of humorous books by Herbert Jenkins—very dated now. Ours belonged to my grandfather. My father loved them too, he was always chuckling. Mrs Bindle always hoped for the best, prepared for the worst, and got caught out by the unexpected. You sound like that.'

Jane pursed her lips. 'Mmm? I always thought pessimists *didn't* hope. But I'll be there.'

Esmeralda chuckled. 'Rory, you're going to be good friends, I can see that. You're already teasing each other. I do hope Jane and her family find a place near here! She and Kate would be great friends, I can see that.'

'I'm sure they would be,' said Adair of Starlight suavely. Jane had an idea he was simply agreeing with Esmeralda. Who was Kate? Fiancée? Wife? Well, whoever she was, she was welcome to this angle-faced stranger.

Jane was at Frankton Arm at seven! She was taking no

chances. Broderic Adair arrived at seven-twenty in a gleaming Daimler-Jag. Jane had expected a rusty, rugged station-wagon. Obviously they belonged to the upper ten of the local farming community. No doubt fluctuating farm prices and markets wouldn't worry them much. Esmeralda sat beside him, beaming, and Jane thought he fussed about her as if she were his own grandmother. He checked that she had heart pills within reach.

Jane couldn't help it. 'It's a bit late for checking that now, isn't it, Mr Adair? You're more than an hour from home, aren't you?'

Esmeralda chuckled. 'He checked there all right. This bit of additional fussiness is to let you know I've angina without stating it baldly. Rory, I'm not sensitive about it. If I feel a pain coming on, I take an angenine tablet and in two shakes of a lamb's tail, I'm okay. They're miracle pills.'

'The thing is, Miss Grey, she's too considerate of other folk, doesn't like slowing them up if the pace is too brisk for her. So watch her.'

Esmeralda pulled a gamine face at him. She really was fun. Broderic inspected the caravan, because that's what it was, an inspection, even if he merely said, 'It's a neat unit. Mind if I have a look inside?' He was obviously making sure his protégée (if anyone Esmeralda's age could be called that) was going to be comfortable. She felt that his approval of the interior, its neatness and obvious adequacy was grudging.

Jane was proud of the caravan. In their last days in Christchurch, Noel had borrowed tools from a friend and contrived wonderful sliding files to hold their canvasses. Everything was shipshape and Bristol fashion. Jane mentioned that. 'Dad wasn't one of your bumbling artists, he couldn't bear to work in a muddle.'

Broderic Adair nodded approvingly. 'That I can approve of. These films one sees of these indescribable garrets with paint-rags cheek-by-jowl with unwashed coffee-cups do nothing for the image of the painting fraternity.'

'You just have to remember,' said Jane, 'that artists vary in temperament and method of operation just as farmers do. On my way here I saw many evidences of that. Some farms as neat as suburban gardens, others bare of as much as a flower, with a hideous jumble of rusting machinery close to the road and dilapidated pioneer cottages in such a state of disrepair that only the hay bales inside seemed to be holding them up. Better by far to raze them to the ground than allow such blots on the landscape.'

'Have you any idea how many thousands of dollars a new hay-shelter costs these days?' demanded Broderic Adair. 'Some farmers can't afford to erect one, so they make use of what shelter they have. They have to feed their stock through drought and severe winters. Farming's like a see-saw these past few years, and it could be a case of having to afford fertilisers and letting new buildings go. Priority is the keyword, and to keep our production up and save the economy.'

Esmeralda burst out laughing. 'Don't worry, Jane. He doesn't live on a farm like that, as I hope you'll see for yourself soon. He'd use up his own last ounce of energy preserving ancient farm buildings in immaculate condition. Rory, you're arguing for arguing's sake. Jane, he's as scathing as you on the subject. A speech of his to the Young Farmers' Club recently was reported in the paper. He said, "Use the old cottages by all means, but keep them in good repair. It pays. And they mustn't be allowed to become eyesores and an affront to the community and tourists alike. Send off outdated machinery to the scrap-iron yards or conceal it behind trees." He also urged them to plant trees for their lives to prevent erosion, to add beauty, and to continue the good work their forefathers did. I must show you some old pictures of Queenstown some time, Jane,' she added. 'The hills surrounding Queenstown Bay were once so bare, so brown. All this,' her eyes swept the piney heights above them lovingly, 'was a case of man enhancing God's handiwork.'

They got Esmeralda settled, but Jane didn't get in beside

her immediately. She walked to the back of the caravan as if to look at something. Broderic took the few steps with her. Jane turned to face him squarely. 'I did this, Mr Adair, so that I could say to you I don't care for your attitude. What's bugging you? Are you possessive about Esmeralda? If so, why? I was delighted to meet her. We are singularly lacking in relations and it was a thrill to find one here, even if only one connected by marriage. It seemed to give her pleasure, too, to find her namesake. I just don't get it . . . your watch-dog air!'

His lip curled. 'Don't you? Are you really so naïve? No one who loves Esmeralda as Kate and I do would welcome any more of the Grey clan crossing her path. Esmeralda is still credulous, still goes on believing in people.'

The wind off the lake blew back the golden-brown tendrils of hair from Jane's broad creamy brow, and the early sun glinted in her eyes and turned them into pure green as they flashed with anger. 'I believe in people too, Mr Adair—even when I meet men like you who seem to look for ulterior motives. Do you think I'm tarred with my grandfather's brush? He was a mean, unloving, tyrannical old man. I want nothing from Esmeralda, if that's what you mean. I just want to give her the affection I'd have given a grandmother, or a godmother.'

'Okay, if it stays that way. As long as you don't regard her as a *fairy* godmother. She hasn't a magic wand or the Midas touch. In fact, she's very poor.'

Jane bit her lip in an effort to restrain herself.

He continued, 'She's been so content these last few years. I want her to stay that way, so don't be like your namesake and leave her life emptier than before.'

Jane's tone was mystified. 'My namesake? What on earth?—I'm Esmeralda's namesake.'

'I mean the Jane Grey bit. Lady Jane Grey was a nine-days' wonder. I can imagine you giving Esmeralda the time of her life for a week or so, then fading out. I don't think you'll find it easy to rent a place round here—besides, it's too chancy expecting sales of pictures to keep four of you. And don't for a moment think Esmeralda got any money from your grandfather—he not only went through all his, he went through hers too.'

Jane went white to her lips. 'You have a horrible mind, quite as horrible as that grandfather of mine you despise! I'm not in the least interested in Esmeralda's money, only in her. Money's not *all*-important in our lives. It's important enough, because my mother and myself have the children to educate. But if my mother had ranked money *all*-important, she'd have married a certain Christchurch business man instead of my own dear stepfather. This man owned three shops. But for one thing she couldn't see him as a good father to me, and for another, she wouldn't marry for security, only for love.

'I recognised Esmeralda as a kindred soul the moment I met her. Now ... she probably thinks you're briefing me still more on her pills and potions, but if we clash swords any longer, she may investigate and it would distress her. I'll see her safely on to the bus after she's had her little holiday with me. Good morning, Mr Adair.'

Jane was past the foot of Lake Hayes and beyond the frowning crags of the Nevis Bluffs before she recovered her good temper, though outwardly she chatted away gaily. Esmeralda was supremely happy. She ought to have had a family of lads and lassies, Jane thought. She was easy on Henry Grey, merely said that he'd been unfortunate with investments for some time. Jane guessed he'd been betting on the horses. It sounded to her as if Esmeralda had sold her lovely home to pay his debts, though she just said she'd found it too large eventually and had taken a small one adjoining the Starlight estate, and had created there a garden which was the darling of her heart.

'There was a shelter-shed at the gates ideal for what I love most to do ... I sell pottery and herbs. Even in winter it's amazing how many tourists pass by, and of course the Kingston Flyer, the old steam-train, attracts so many people to the area. It runs from Lumsden to Kingston, reminiscent of the old days when there was no road from the foot of the lake to Frankton. The Devil's Staircase blocked the road project till about 1936. Tourists came from Invercargill to Kingston, then took one of the lake-steamers to Queenstown. Anthony Trollope did, you know.'

Jane was astounded. 'Anthony Trollope, the Victorian novelist? Of the *Pallisers* TV series? Truly?'

'Yes, then he and his wife, Rose Trollope, came through these gorges, in snow, by coach.'

'Oh, how fascinating, Godmother! I know so little of this history, beyond a few stories of the gold-rush. I do plan to study it. I think it could help me get the feeling of the terrain I'm painting, to know its historical background. Esmeralda, tell me about your little house.'

Esmeralda chuckled. 'Well, it's not really little, for a start, but was cheaper because it hadn't been used for so long, and of course it had to be renovated a bit. It really needed reconstruction, which would have cost the earth, but it has an air about it. The tennis-court was in good repair, and the swimming-pool, so I made this available to the young fry of the district, and their parents keep it in trim. So I'm never lonely. The pool has a safety fence round, so I planted it with roses and clematis and put a deep herbaceous border there, beginning with Canterbury bells and delphiniums, perennial phlox, Michaelmas daisies, larkspur, peonies, right down to primroses and *bellis perennis*, which I prefer to call double daisies, at the edge. Starlight Peaks rise above that long line of colour, and people from all over the world have exclaimed at its beauty. There's a spinney at one end of larches and birches, and a pine-wood, and I kept the swings and jungle-bars for the children.'

It must have been some place in its palmy days, thought Jane. It would be an old pioneer house, fallen on hard times.

'The children had made little paths everywhere, following the natural contours of the hillside and stream, around the rocks,' Esmeralda went on. 'So I fringed those paths with flowers and shrubs and named them all ... there's the Hydrangea Walk, the Catmint Path, the Azalea Bend, and the Lilac Way has bushes in purple, lilac, and white. I have little box hedges too. The road verge is a mass of Russell lupins in all colours, from November through till late January, and it's so sheltered I can grow fuchsias, even though in winter the mountains around us are thick with snow for months. I've a tangle of native bush and I've named all the trees in it with both their Maori and botanical names—Rory painted them in black on white wood. All along the Adair water I have irises, and in spring, now, there are hundreds of daffodils, narcissi and snowdrops. Rory built me a curved stone bridge over it. He can turn his hand to anything. The birdsong sounds from morning till night. I've never regretted my up-to-the-minute residence in Queenstown. This is something I created myself.

'I painted the doors of the house pale green and white; that Wedgwood green. Rory immediately called it the Wedgwood House, so we use that as the name of my wee shop too. They are those old-fashioned doors with four inset panels surrounded by the white moulding. Rory put up rough saplings for a rustic pergola along the path in front of the house, and roofed it in with that transparent roofing, and I eat out there a lot. I have Shot Silk pink roses climbing up the saplings, and tubs of ivy geranium and purple verbena. The whole world comes to my door, even from Alaska and Russia. It's a funny old place, but it's mine. No place like home.'

A yearning for just a place for the four of them to call home twisted Jane's heart. Most of all for Mother, who wasn't so young any more and who had known so little of security in her life.

They came out of the awesome grandeur of the Gorge and turned left for Wanaka. The road stretched before them with mountains almost purple with distance, reaching into infinity and beginning at Lake Hawea, Esmeralda said. The hillsides that Jane remembered as lion-gold in the parched conditions of the autumn were emerald now, and everywhere the apple and stone-fruit orchards were drifts of pink-and-white blossom. A fair and lovely land.

The bulk of Mount Iron, guardian bluff of Lake Wanaka, came into view and they swung round to meet the cornflower blue of this lake with its gentler outlines, rimmed with mountains, Black Peak thrusting through its cape of snow, way back in the Matukituki Valley.

They called at the little shop Jane was to share with an arts-and-crafts display, then went on round the lake-front to the camping-ground and plugged the van in. Esmeralda proved to be entranced with caravan living. Jane promised her a longer holiday in it in time to come. 'If at all possible we want to keep it. It's the only way we could afford family holidays, and with Dad fitting it up like this for painting forays, I tell myself it's a justifiable indulgence. Mum's got the wee Mini she had in Fiji. If we have to sell it for a deposit on a house, we will, but I'd rather rent a place till I prove I can sell all year round here.'

Esmeralda approved this. She was a great sales booster too. She knew so many lakeside people that she soon passed the word around and they had a most profitable five days. Then they went house-hunting.

The story was the same, in slightly lesser degree, as in Queenstown. The holiday homes, naturally, would be let only on a short term basis, so they could command the bigger prices in the school vacations. In desperation Jane toured the area from the Cardrona Valley to beyond Hawea and Tarras, looking hungrily at every farm that held more than one farm cottage, calling on the off-chance that they employed casual labour and had quarters to spare.

On the last day of her search they drove back to the caravan, depressed. At least Jane was.

Suddenly Esmeralda's eyes lit up. Why? 'Jane, child, this gives me the courage to propose something. I didn't earlier, as I thought your mother would prefer to be completely on her own with her family, but I would so like you near me.

24

Wedgwood House is so large; share it with me. When I first went there, before I worked up such a good connection for pottery and herbs, I used to rent out the part I didn't use in summer, so it has two kitchens—and four entrances in all. It can be completely separate. That way your mother wouldn't worry lest the children were too much for me. I admit they might be if I had them all the time. I'm eighty, but I feel good enough for another decade, but that same decade's going to be a problem if I'm living on my own. With you through a communicating door I could live out there as long as I've got. I've such a dread of finishing up in a home in Invercargill away from my mountains. But if you were with me it'd save Rory this continual popping-in to see if I'm all right. He's a good lad, that.'

Jane hadn't liked what she'd seen of him this far, but per-perhaps his very anxiety for Esmeralda was commendable; he'd seen her taken advantage of by Jane's own grand-father. He'd soon realise they weren't at all like Henry.

Jane cupped her hands about her chin, propped her elbows on the table and stared excitedly at her step-grandmother. 'Oh, darling, are you sure? I mean, for us it would be ideal, in spite of what——' She stopped short.

The beautiful blue eyes looking into hers looked puzzled. 'In spite of what, child?'

Jane knew she mustn't make mischief. She said swiftly, 'In spite of feeling that the day of miracles is over.'

Esmeralda accepted that, her eyes dreamy. 'It will be wonderful. You can display your paintings in my shop where all the world goes by. Not only motorists, either. Sometimes they put on a bus-load from Kingston for the ones who come up by the flyer, to visit my crafts centre. The days you go painting, your mother and myself can tend the shop. And sometimes I have a neighbour come in, as now, so we aren't tied to it. The school bus passes the door and takes the children to the school at Athol. That's been the story for years since the Maunga-Whetu school closed.'

'Maunga-Whetu? Is that the name of the township?'

'Yes, it's tiny, just a village really, but serves a large area. It means the Mountain of the Stars. *Maunga* is mountain. *Whetu* is star. There's just the church, the store, a garage. Jane, what will your mother say? She may not want to have anything to do with someone bearing your grandfather's name.'

Jane was frank. 'She *could* feel that . . . till she meets you. I'd like her to meet you first, then be told about the relationship. Would you be willing at first meeting to be just someone I met and liked and who has a house divided into two flats? Grey isn't an uncommon name, and I wouldn't mention the Esmeralda at first. Then she'd have no preconceived reservations.'

Esmeralda shook her head. 'No, it's too risky. She'd feel she'd been conned into something; she must know. She's only at Oamaru. How about my accompanying you? It wouldn't only give her a chance to look me over, but it would give you time for second thoughts.'

Jane kissed her. 'How wise! That's the difference between being twenty-four and having reached the age of wisdom . . .'

Esmeralda looked rueful, and, for a moment, incredibly young. 'Mmm. But at sixty-nine, when I should have been able to curb my native impetuosity, I got bowled over by meeting Henry again and married him.' She looked back into a sadder past, sighed, then brightened. 'But it's brought me you, so I'll not rue it.'

Jane felt a wave of love rise up and swamp her. 'I'll ring Mother tonight, that'll give her two days to get used to the idea. Godmother, would you like to ring Broderic Adair?'

A naughty twinkle lit Esmeralda's eyes. 'No, just before we leave for Oamaru I'll merely wire him that I'm off to meet my new family.'

Jane summed it up mentally. Esmeralda would wire him at the last possible moment so that he wouldn't try to contact her at the camp and dissuade her. It was no earthly business of Adair of Starlight, but Jane was pretty sure he wouldn't want them living on his doorstep. She wouldn't say anything to Mother or the girls .·. . this was one battle she could fight herself.

CHAPTER TWO

JANE's mother had news of her own to impart before she could get one word out. 'Jane darling, I was dying for you to be in touch. I've got a temporary job nurse-aiding in an old folks' home here, a marvellous one. It will save us dipping into our savings. Also, Mrs Greenwell can let us have this flat as long as we like and she's reduced the rent a little, because she's so pleased with the way we've got the garden in order. Now, don't feel too badly if you haven't found us a cottage, it's not as urgent as it was.'

Jane told her what had happened, said she was bringing Esmeralda for a holiday with them, and added that she'd leave the final decision to her mother. 'But having this established craft centre would be super, and it would be of benefit to her too, having a family under her roof, yet with their own separate quarters. You'll be able to use her wheel and kiln.'

Willy Eastwood was a little cautious, said it sounded just great, but that they'd have to see. However, once she met Esmeralda, her reservations melted like snow on the Remarkables in a nor'wester. Louise and Lauris took to her on sight. 'We've never had a grandmother,' Lauris informed her, 'and you're exactly like a picture-book one with pink cheeks and blue eyes and white hair done up on top, yet in outlook you're really with it.'

Louise added, 'We're awfully short on relations. My best friend in Fiji was one of ten, and the fun they had you wouldn't believe, and they had six grandparents.'

Esmeralda blinked. 'Six? Well, the good Lord certainly provided well for that family. How come?'

'Well, two were great-grandparents, but not married to each other, if you get me.'

Esmeralda said she understood perfectly. 'It must be that one on each side was widowed.'

Jane chuckled. 'You're going to be a real acquisition to this family, Godmother. Anyone who can fathom the twins' conversation must have a really high I.Q.!'

Louise said, heaving a sigh, 'It's a great disability being a twin. One loses one's individual personality. People will talk about you as if you were . . . um . . . inanimate objects.'

Jane's eyes bulged. 'Inanimate? Good heavens! From the moment you were born, you were complete jitterbugs, always on the go, with three of us after you every moment of the day.'

Lauris flew to Louise's defence. 'You know exactly what she means. People say "the twins" as if they were talking about "the tables" or "the chairs"—it—er—what's the word I want? It minimises our personality.'

Esmeralda turned a laugh into a cough most adroitly. Jane said, 'As if anything short of a steamroller could do that! And you're doing the same thing yourself. You said *our* personality, so if *you* can't separate yourselves, why should we?'

Louise gazed on Esmeralda appreciatively. 'But already you make us feel like . . . like . . . um——'

'Separate entities,' suggested Esmeralda, knitting-needles clicking on a ski-cap she was making.

Louise beamed. 'I couldn't have put it better myself. We were lucky, though, that Mum and Dad didn't believe in twins being dressed alike, and also in not being identical.'

'You're not alone in being thankful for that,' said Jane, 'if we'd not been able to tell you apart when it came to apportioning blame, life would have been even more difficult.'

'She just talks like that,' Lauris assured Esmeralda. 'We don't take it to heart. She's quite fond of us. It's the generation gap.'

Esmeralda was wiping tears away. 'That puts you on the shelf, Jane! I've not laughed so much for years. Oh, how thankful I am I found you. I feel ten years younger. By the end of the year I'll be skipping about like a mountain goat!'

By now, their mother was so drawn to Esmeralda that she felt the whole thing had been providential, and this was largely due to the way the old lady treated the twins. She didn't talk down to them, was endlessly patient, yet never allowed them to get above themselves, and when the twins asked her if they could call her Granny, her cup of happiness was full. She thought being called Granny was something to have been denied her.

Now she said crisply, 'Mind you, you can do the bobbles for your ski-caps. Lauris, would you like red intermingled with this emerald green? I know Louise wants white in her blue. Mind you don't have any lordly ideas about skiing, though, just because next winter you'll be living in the snow-sports area. It's a very expensive sport. You'll have to earn yourselves some money this summer to be able to afford even the occasional day up at the ski-grounds. There's so much to pay for—hire of ski-boots and skis, chairlifts and so on, to say nothing of the bus-fares up to Coronet Peak, though to be sure Rory will take you up sometimes. He's got a four-wheel drive and is an expert on chains. He's also a fine skier, having lived there all his life, but he's not a fanatic. Farmers rarely are—haven't the time.'

'Who's Rory? What a gorgeous name! Is he young and handsome and redheaded? Rorys always ought to be red-headed.' This from Louise.

Jane said dryly, 'You're completely off beam. He's dark chestnut, but a very dark-visaged man, with a scowl to match and——'

Esmeralda chuckled. 'Jane didn't see him at his best. He regarded her with suspicion, as a flibbertigibbet artist, carrying off an octogenarian with as little thought as if she'd have asked a teenager to have a holiday in the van. He fussed round like a maiden aunt and put her back up. When he sees how much weight I've put on and how happy I am, they'll be the best of friends. It will relieve him of so much of the responsibility of having someone so aged living on his doorstep.'

Lauris asked, 'Is Wedgwood House on his property, then?'

Jane knew apprehension. She'd not thought of that. Fancy living with these adventurous twins on Broderic Adair's land! To be fair, it wouldn't be easy for him. It was one thing to have an aged, but dear, friend living there, and quite another to have two exuberant eleven-year-olds swarming over it.

Esmeralda said, 'In the early pioneer days it was part of the Kingston run. Gradually the estate got whittled down, and now the run is even smaller. Rory lost a fair slice of it when a new road was put through a year or two ago.'

Jane imagined just how Adair of Starlight would have reacted to that. She could picture Broderic striding about, consumed with anger ... probably even bearding the Government lions in their lair at Parliament House in Wellington before he caved in to the inevitable.

She took a mental pull on herself. This was stupid! She couldn't remember, ever, feeling such antagonism towards a man. She mustn't encourage this. Broderic Adair was probably right to be suspicious of the sudden appearance of the granddaughter of the man who'd run through his friend's money and rendered her old age less bountiful, but Mother would disarm him. When he saw how well they were looking after Esmeralda, he might live to be thankful. Meanwhile the girls went on asking all the questions Jane had disdained to ask. 'What's his wife like? Has he any children our age?'

'No, he's not married yet, but it's time he was, he's over thirty. He's been running the estate for years. His parents retired early because their elder daughter, Isabel, was widowed early in life, and was teaching in Wanganui. They took a farmlet on the outskirts of that city and built Isabel a small house on the same property, and it means they're always there for the children.

31

'But there are children on the estate just the same, Josef Stewart and Gretchen. Their mother is an Austrian. She came out for a holiday years ago with her brother who was a ski-instructor, and she and Hamish fell in love with each other. There's also a fat roly-poly baby called Sholto. Lisel said it was only fair that one of their children should have a Scots name. Josef would be about your age. Gretchen is nine.'

Jane said, 'You mentioned a Kate. Is she Broderic Adair's fiancée?'

'No, his younger sister. She's in the North Island too—a physiotherapist at Palmerston North, so not too far from the rest of the family. She's at the stage where a change would do her good, though. She's been up there some years.' She paused and added, 'So she's coming home soon to keep house for Rory.'

She hadn't known the twins long enough to realise how astute they were. Louise clasped her hands together and sighed rapturously, 'She's coming home to nurse a broken heart!'

Esmeralda looked startled. 'Well, that about sums it up, but she's a sensible gal and probably wouldn't put it quite like that.'

Louise and Lauris exchanged speculative looks. Lauris nodded as if she knew what Louise was thinking. 'And she'll find that after all, she loves the boy next door.'

Esmeralda laughed. She'd laughed a lot since coming here. 'There isn't a next door. Just mountains and a deep valley behind you; the road round the lake to Queenstown goes past our front gate to the north; the road to Lake Te Anau and Fiordland goes to the south, and to the west, in front, is range upon range, valley upon valley. Still, when Kate gets over this, no doubt she'll find someone else. No, girls, it's Kate's business and Kate's alone, and I'm not going to gossip about it. To get back to our muttons, about earning enough for skiing costs, I've no doubt Rory will find you a job at Starlight.'

Over my dead body, thought Jane. She was busy enough while the girls were at school and Mother nursing. She shut herself into her tiny sun-porch for hours at a time, working on the sketches she'd brought back with her. She had only to shut her eyes to see the colours and contours of that glorious countryside. She had a small transformer fitted to her slide-viewer and constantly referred to it for certain lights and shadows. Esmeralda said that she and her mother would be able to have a studio each at the Wedgwood House.

Esmeralda had reluctantly agreed to them renting their half, so their future looked bright. The month rolled on. Esmeralda didn't seem much of a letter-writer, merely sending off the occasional postcard to Adair. Jane was surprised that two or three quite lengthy letters came from him in that time; he was more like a son than a neighbour. Esmeralda read them aloud to the family. If Jane hadn't met him she'd have thought him a pleasant fellow to keep an old lady *au fait* with all the local happenings.

The lambing was almost over, he said. A good year, few losses. 'We missed you, of course, for mothering some of the orphans, but as usual Lisel mucked in. The kids are earning extra money feeding your fowls. The bantams are waxing extra fat. Why is it that kids can't help favouring bantams? They always get the extra handful of wheat. I hinted that those bantams were past their best laying days, and the kids fell on me tooth and nail like anti-euthanasia protesters.

'Josef is taking more interest in his homework and Lisel puts it down to the fact that I've been staying on after dinner and he's allowed to carry on with the German lessons Lisel started me on, if he gets his homework done first. Between that and TV it fills in the evenings I used to spend with you. Glad you're enjoying Oamaru, but when are you coming home? Don't overdo. You're pretty spry for your age, Esmeralda, but your inability to realise you're not a giddy young thing in your twenties any more puts you at risk. Don't forget good people are scarce.

'I took, or rather guided, a party from a North Island naturalists' club up past the Giant's Causeway last Saturday. We borrowed a few more four-wheel drive vehicles as some of them weren't exactly spring chickens, and took them as far as Miners' Diversion. But they were surprisingly fit. And *did* they know their stuff? Most could fit names to every alpine plant they encountered. Their reaction to the scenery was most satisfying—not that it could be anything else. I may have lived with it all my life, but the view from the edge is breathtaking. And there was a rainbow springing out of the Never-never-land as a bonus. They came back to the homestead for their evening meal and I showed slides of the area. Rob and Stella brought the provisions. They were staying at Drumlogie.'

Esmeralda looked over her spectacles at them. 'Robert Adair is an uncle of Rory's and Stella is his wife. They run this guesthouse back along the Gorge Road from Queenstown, towards Moonlight, in conjunction with their son and Giles Logie. You'll probably get invited there. Stella's older grandchildren are about your age.'

She went on reading: 'Josef and Gretchen got special prizes at the school pet-show for Minto and Pinto. First time we've shown donkeys and believe me, it will be the last. They just wouldn't go in the floats, and it finished up with Hamish and me riding those thrice-accursed animals to the show and the kids gave us an ovation when we arrived and about ninety per cent of them had cameras! Hamish didn't look so bad, his legs didn't scrape the ground once, but I looked idiotic and my shoes were ruined.'

Two pairs of awed and delighted eyes gazed at Esmeralda. 'Donkeys! How absolutely super. He'll let us ride them, won't he? And doesn't he sound fun?' Jane admitted he did, but——

Lauris said, disappointed, as the letter finished, 'He doesn't mention us coming. How strange.'

34

Esmeralda said evasively, 'Well, I thought I'd just tell him when I got home. You can't get much on a postcard.'

Lauris disapproved. 'I'm sure he must have looked for a letter from you. He must be lonely. But not when we get there, eh?'

Jane's voice was dry. 'You mustn't imagine you'll be allowed to swarm all over Starlight, Lauris. It'd be different for the Stewart children, they live there. You'll wait till you're asked.'

'Oh, don't fash yourself,' said Esmeralda, 'Rory's good with children, though he never lets them get above themselves.'

'I'll bet he doesn't,' thought Jane, 'and he'll think we're imposing on Esmeralda as it is. That's why she's not told him yet. Anyway, it's not really safe for her to live alone.' But she couldn't rid herself of the thought that he was going to disapprove.

Came the day Esmeralda announced she must go home. Jane said, 'I've been worrying about you changing buses in Dunedin. I'll run you to Dunedin in Mum's Mini and put you on the Queenstown one. You'll be met at the other end, won't you?'

'Yes, Rory would meet me, but I've a better idea. If you took me down, had a look at the accommodation and did some painting, it would help you get your stock up. You could put some of your pictures in the van, because I'm pretty sure you'll stay. You might even be able to sell some of those you have already framed.'

Mother beamed. 'It would be ideal. I'd like to keep this job going as long as it lasts, though it'll be heaven to come to Maunga-Whetu and get going on my own thing again. I'd really like, if possible, to stay here till the school year finishes in December; less than two months to go. The twins ought not to have another move so soon.'

So the canvasses were slotted in, the caravan packed. Mother was sure they were doing the right thing, and said she'd have their goods in Auckland storage sent down to Dunedin and thence to Queenstown.

Esmeralda nodded. 'Good idea, because I just furnished the rooms for holiday letting with what I had, and your things will make it more homely.'

Louise nodded. 'And we've lots of native matting, lovely for a studio because you can scrub paint off it, and some of it would look lovely in the shop, to set off the pottery.'

'Because it's handmade,' said Lauris sagely, 'and that goes with jars and lavender bags. Tourists just mop up such stuff.'

'There is no doubt,' said Esmeralda, 'that these two know their onions. They've lots of horse-sense, and that's a commodity no one can get along well without. Rory Adair is going to approve of you, I can feel it in my bones.'

Jane reflected that what *she* felt in *her* bones was that Rory Adair was going to feel his territory was being invaded by a monstrous army of women.

They set off on a glorious late October day, through the rolling North Otago countryside. Now and then Jane drew into the side and sketched some endearing formation that had caught her trained eye . . . a road curving up a hill, with a weathered limestone stable clustered about with elderberries in creamy blossom, or guarded by poplars in full leaf, reaching like spires to the cloudless blue.

They went inland from Palmerston along the Pigroot, to bypass Dunedin and come into Central at Alexandra, not as scenic a route as from Milton, but with a desolate grandeur all its own. Then after their picnic lunch they were into the gorges, first the Cromwell, then the Kawarau, with massive rock walls narrowing each side of them, making Jane feel that they were shut into a world of swirling green waters carving and gouging out their turbulent way year after remorseless year. As they neared the end of the Kawarau, Jane knew a moment of quite unreasonable fear of the future. As if this rugged scenery somehow threatened her; as if it bred men as harsh, yet strangely attractive . . . one in particular,

Broderic Adair, who would, she knew, resent them, regarding them as spongers upon the bounty of an old woman who had already given one member of their family her all.

She pulled herself together. The blue gleam of the lake came into view beneath its classical mountains. Frankton was almost level, with holiday homes on terraces gently sloping down to a boat harbour. They crossed the Kawarau bridge, skirted the river on the far side, went through an over-arching tunnel of huge English trees, then headed south beneath the awesomely jagged heights of the Remarkables, under which stud Herefords grazed, and a wistaria-wreathed homestead with a moon-gate as entrance to its swimming-pool, added its own beauty to the scene.

The road wound beside the lake for miles and miles, with very few homesteads beside it on the lower slopes of the mountains this side. Across the waters that were pale azure today, the over-lake heights came steeply down to the edges, with very few beaches, and looked completely untenanted; although one or two homesteads, reached only by launches, were tucked into the valleys.

It was late afternoon before they saw the little hamlet of Kingston nestling at the foot of the lake, and then the mountains parted a little. When they passed the signpost to Fairlight Esmeralda said 'Not far now,' and in no time a broad sash of rainbow colours on the road-verge struck the eye with loveliness, in a profusion of Russell lupins. The pine-slab shelter behind it bore the legend *The Wedgwood Green Crafts Centre.*

Lombardy poplars and aspen poplars rustling in soft wind-music sheltered it, and on the mown green oval of turf in front of the little shop were silver birches dotted about, a weeping elm bending under a weight of pale green blossom, an ash filtering sunlight through its leaves and a circular seat under every tree, a place that invited cars to stop.

Jane looked up behind the stall to the rise, expecting to see some gracious old homestead saved from years of neglect. Instead she saw a building that had undoubtedly been a school, but it must be the Green Wedgwood House all right, because its doors were that delicate shade of green, piped with white moulding.

A country school of the old days, all Esmeralda could afford when Henry Grey went through her money. A small-ish place as a school, but a big place to live in. It was barn-like and no architectural gem, but Esmeralda's garden had softened the harshness and flung a garland of colour about its utility lines.

That would be why Esmeralda had called the wayside stall a shelter-shed. In the old days schools had these for the children to crowd into at playtimes and lunch-hours when it rained. Jane didn't think that Esmeralda had pur-posely disguised the true nature of the house to her. She was alert in mind for her age, but no doubt her memory played her tricks at times, and she must have thought she'd mentioned it. This explained the swimming-pool, the tennis-court, the swings and jungle-bars.

Never mind, no matter how odd the interior would be, and it could hardly be anything else, it was a roof over their heads. Oh, how happy the children would be here in this alpine air, what freedom for their ramblings . . . what peace, what singing happiness of birdsong and brook they would have all about them.

She turned to Esmeralda and said in tones so appreciative that the old lady couldn't have guessed at her disappoint-ment, 'You've created a dream out of what must have been bare playgrounds and hillside. I didn't dream it would be like this, all colour and scent. And what views we'll have!'

Esmeralda nodded, content. Her darling Jane liked it. 'They built the school on the rise so that when the winter snows thawed they would drain away. That's why the roof's so steep. It's as good as the day it was built. I've never known it to leak, even in the worst of storms, and the walls are sturdy too, and the windows draught-proof.'

Jane quoted softly, 'The beams of our house are cedar, and our rafters of fir.' As Esmeralda turned an enchanted face towards her, a shadow fell upon Jane, cutting off the sunlight. She turned. Broderic Adair!

He looked at her strangely, she thought. He said, 'Call me a purist if you like, but the beams are *kauri* and the rafters *rimu*. They built their schools well in those days and New Zealand *kauri* is one of the most durable woods in the world.'

She felt puzzled, then understood. 'Oh, Mr Adair, do you think I wouldn't know that? Do you think I'm Fijian and will know only bamboo and palms and other flimsy materials? I was born and bred in Christchurch, and didn't see Fiji till I was twelve. I was merely quoting the Bible, the Song of Solomon.'

'My apologies. I did think just that. I'm rather given to imparting information gratis, owing to living in a tourist area, and I'm apt to give answers before the questions are framed.' He kissed Esmeralda. 'You look so well, your holiday must have agreed with you. You're positively blooming.'

Well, that was something! Esmeralda said, 'So I should be. I had breakfast in bed every morning and a warm fire to get up to, and the sort of meals you can have with five of a family. What fun those girls are, Louise and Lauris. I never laughed so much in my life. And Willy is so sweet. She made me so welcome.'

'Willy? *She?* Who——'

'Jane's mother, Henry's daughter-in-law. Just the sort of daughter-in-law I'd have longed for had I had a son. She was June Willymore before she married, and became Grey, and began painting as June Grey. Then she married Noel Eastwood, but you wouldn't want two painters called Eastwood, so she kept to Grey, but when Jane became an artist, June was too like Jane, so Jane put Esmeralda on hers. Wasn't that providential?'

Broderic Adair put a hand to his head. 'You've lost me, I'm afraid. Why did she have to put Esmeralda and where does the hand of Providence come in?'

Esmeralda said placidly, 'Men aren't so quick on the uptake as women. I said because June's too like Jane, and if she hadn't used her second name I'd never have guessed she was my own kin.'

Jane, watching Broderic's expression, had a fair idea that he thought Providence hadn't had much to do with it; more like the Devil himself!

He said nothing to that, but went on, 'Mrs Daniel had to close the shop early today, but I've just said goodbye to a bunch of tourists who were pretty free spenders. Aunt Stella rang up from Drumlogie to say they wanted herbs and pottery, and she'd keep them to half an hour. I was taking the money up to the homestead for you, it's safer there.'

Esmeralda thanked him for sparing the time, then, 'I'll show Jane the shop later. She's had a long day driving. I'd like her to have a meal and a rest now.'

He nodded. 'Good of you to bring Mrs Grey home. It'll have taken up a couple of days of your time, and I do appreciate it.'

Nicely said, but the nuance was there, and Jane got it. She was the newcomer in Esmeralda's life. Her old friend was making it sound like a favour done to a stranger, not to a near-grandmother. She wished Esmeralda had already told him what was afoot.

She said, 'Mr Adair, I think I'd better tell——'

Esmeralda interrupted. 'Jane child, don't be so formal. Seeing you're going to be close neighbours, you'd better make it Rory from the start.'

The dark brows twitched together. 'Neighbours? *Close* neighbours? What's going on?'

Esmeralda looked innocent. 'Oh, yes, I meant to say on my card, but there wasn't room. Jane tried for a cottage further afield, but it was hopeless, so I've offered them the holiday half of the school.'

Jane saw the dark face tighten. He said, 'There was nothing offering anywhere? What about Hawea and Tarras?'

She said, 'I tried everywhere, the Cardrona, Luggate, Albertown, even calling on any farm we saw with cottages

40

in the hope one might be empty. We've a flat in Oamaru, but we must be in the centre of the tourist industry.'

'Of course, and Esmeralda can lay it all on for you, the room, the position, the already established Crafts Centre.' It was said smoothly.

Esmeralda said happily, 'Yes, wasn't it fortuitous?'

'Very.' Again the dry note.

Esmeralda continued, 'And of course having paintings here will increase my trade too, and having company in the house will lessen your responsibility towards me, Rory.'

A smile lit his face. 'Since when have I ever found you a burden, Esmeralda?'

The old lady gave him a look of pure comradeship. Whatever his faults, she looked upon him as the grandson she'd never had. 'Rory . . . never. But that doesn't stop me from being glad that now the task can be shared.'

'But when Kate comes home, it'll be shared in any case.'

'I'll enjoy that, but Jane and her family will be sleeping here.'

'True. Well, I'll go on up. Where are you going to put the caravan? You'll find the garage high enough. I used to keep one of the trucks there.'

Jane hoped he'd go to his own place, or to the Stewarts if they were cooking his evening meal. He didn't. By the time he'd got the caravan into the garage, he was standing beside the green-and-white doors and had flung them both open.

It was the strangest feeling, stepping into a school corridor. It had stone flagging, and a strip of carpet-runner down the middle. All along the row of windows was a deep sill, obviously added, and it was filled with pot-plants, busy Lizzies, ivies, primulas, African violets, fuchsias, ferns.

Esmeralda looked up to see a row of wire baskets filled with peat and hanging plants and exclaimed, 'Oh, Rory, you dear boy, you've got them up for me. How it softens that high ceiling! But what's the cord by each?'

He grinned. 'A pulley. See, I've invented a catch, foolproof I hope, to hold each one down, because I've no faith at all in your promise to let me climb up for the watering.'

Jane knew a softening. That was a big thing for a busy farmer to do, to please an old lady. He could easily have thought she had enough plants outdoors to satisfy her.

When Esmeralda had done oohing and aahing, she opened the door into what had been a big classroom but had been cunningly divided with a built-in wall with an arched open-ing to connect them, and with a concertina door to close when cosiness was desirable. Half was dining-room, half lounge.

It was carpeted wall-to-wall, so Grandfather couldn't have reduced Esmeralda to absolute poverty; a softly muted carpet in greys and lavender and rose, and the loose covers on the old-fashioned furniture, deep and comfortable, were in the same tonings, repeating the colours of the herbaceous border.

A big fireplace was piled high with cones, awaiting a match, and Broderic bent down to light it. 'I'll bring you down milk and something for your meal. How about centre-loin chops, quick and easy to do? Your mail is on the desk. By the way,' he turned to Jane, 'when do you intend to settle in as a family?'

'I'm staying now. Mother is working and wants the twins to finish the school year in Oamaru. They've had enough upheaval for one year. We came to Auckland first, then south.'

'Why here, particularly?'

'Because Dad and I had planned that. We came here pro-specting. He fell in love with this scenery and felt he could make good here, only—he didn't live to make his dream come true.'

His voice was a little softer, she granted him that. 'I see. Tough luck. It's a wonder, though, you didn't just stay on in Fiji.'

'Mother prefers a more bracing climate—she was born in Christchurch. Besides, I too, as well as Noel, felt I'd found

42

my métier here. If the way our pictures sold in Queenstown and Wanaka was just a flash in the pan, I'll work in one of the hotels. I did a lot of waitressing in Fiji, acted as a receptionist, chambermaid, the lot. But here, with the Crafts Centre at the very gate, I should make a go of it.'

'Especially with free quarters thrown in,' he agreed suavely.

Jane's chin came up, but before she could speak, Esmeralda did. She didn't sound defensive, only rueful. 'She won't take them for free. Her mother won't hear of it either. They had to be talked into accepting my offer even at a rent; they were afraid it might upset my quiet way of life. The rooms would be far better occupied. They're even metered for separate power accounts.'

Jane got in before he could speak. 'I'm afraid we made a compromise there, Mr Adair—all right, Godmother, I'll make it Broderic! I'm aware it's only a nominal rent at the moment, but we've agreed that if I have a good season, we'll adjust that at New Year. Is that all right with you?'

The last question was meant to be sarcastic, because what had it to do with Broderic Adair who wasn't even connected with Esmeralda by marriage, but it misfired. He took it as his right, nodded, said, 'Yes, it can be adjusted later.'

She was suddenly tired of this and dispirited. She said with sincerity, 'I think my godmother looks as if she needs a hot drink. This basket's got some milk over from our lunch; I'll make some tea right away and cook our meal later. Perhaps to save you coming back with the chops, I could come for them if you tell me where. A good walk would be fine after that drive.'

'Depends what you call a good walk. It's only up through the fir-wood past the garage, a clearly defined path, then turn uphill a little, through a spinney of larches and birches, and the house is right there. That's a good idea.'

Jane wondered why. Then it hit her. He wanted to see her alone when there need be no holds barred for fear of distressing Esmeralda. She knew beyond a shadow of doubt that he didn't want any of them at Starlight. Well, it would take more than antagonism from a dark-avised stranger to winkle her out of this ideal setting. As far as she was concerned it was an answer to prayer.

He refused the cup Esmeralda offered him, praise be. Jane got the old lady comfortably ensconced in one of the deep wing chairs, found a footstool for her feet. Esmeralda chuckled, 'I bid fair to be spoilt! I'd not realised how wonderful it was to have a goddaughter. I can take a lot of this. Now, when I've finished I'll just lie back and doze. I've had a wonderful day. After all that company in Oamaru I'd have been a lonely old woman coming home by myself.'

At any other time Jane would have delighted in this woodland path, the artist in her appreciating the dappled shade of leaves and sun on the beaten ash-white path, the colours of the lichens patching the rocks with russet and lime and sulphur, the little creeping mosses and tiny alpine meadow plants, but she was too tense. However, she wouldn't stay that way. Their presence at Wedgwood House was nothing to do with Mr Curmudgeon Adair!

She came up a bank where wild thyme gave out a fragrance as her feet crushed it, a tall girl in tan-coloured trews and an emerald green tank top tucked in at a slim belted waist, and she gave no hint of how fast her heart was beating beneath it. She whistled as she came. Pooh to Broderic Adair!

She rounded a clump of lilac and there before her was Starlight Homestead, with all the lovely lines she'd not found in the school conversion, with a dear, irregular garden growing round its natural rock formations and surging in an irrepressible tide of colour and scent right up to its front loggia that was wreathed with plumy wistaria. It looked as if, like Topsy, it had 'just growed'. It was so right for its setting, and just breathed of solid secure things, with probably four generations of Adairs rooted and grounded in stable and enduring comfort. People like this had no idea what it was to have no real security behind

44

them. All Jane wanted was a family rooftree.

Children, from pioneer days on, had peered out from those dormer windows ... little boys in sailor suits and girls in white embroidered pinafores and button boots had chased each other in and out of the copsy corners of the garden, played hide-and-seek and bar-the-door. In the long southern twilight, couples had no doubt courted on that loggia, half-screened behind the pink roses and the wistaria; grandparents had rocked in those ancient chairs.

Jane took a resolve ... she'd work unsparingly at her easel. If her pictures became popular she'd make far more than ever she could washing dishes or waiting on tables. She must make money quickly so that some day she could pay a deposit on a cottage somewhere in this area, and be dependent upon no one's bounty, nor the target of veiled remarks from a hostile man ...

Broderic Adair came out on to the steps, waited for her. She held her head high, met his hazel eyes under their dark reddish brows fearlessly. His expression was unreadable as he led the way in.

It was a lovely home and someone must come in to do for him, Jane thought, for except that there were no flowers in the vases, the woodwork was well polished and dusted. That urn would look lovely with flax leaves and their big black flower-stalks in it, mixed with golden rod and montbrietia. Heavens, what was she thinking?

The kitchen wasn't so tidy. Boots caked with dry mud stood in one corner and a few tools lay on the table. But there were no unwashed dishes. A basket stood on the bench and held bottles of milk, butter, brown eggs, a loaf, some fruit and the chops.

Broderic Adair sat on the corner of the table, folded his arms across his massive chest, looked at her consideringly. Jane took an exquisite pleasure in removing the loaf, the butter, the fruit. 'I bought all of these in Alexandra as we came through, thank you, but Esmeralda said not to bother with eggs. I stocked up on other things too, sausages among them, but the chops will be nicer.'

'You do cook, then?'

Jane widened her eyes. 'But of course. Why wouldn't I? Oh, I get it. You think artists are impractical people—how very naïve of you! I don't just slap up Fijian dishes either, curries, with coconut and spices, and tropical fruit salads . . . Esmeralda just delighted in my mother's steamed puddings and pies, and her roast beef and Yorkshire puddings; the things a woman on her own wouldn't cook, naturally. I think your protégée will be looked after better than for many a day, Mr Adair. You give me the impression you think we're on the make.'

'And aren't you?' he asked coolly. 'Nothing that's happened so far has caused me to think you're likely to be any different from the importunate Mr Grey our dear impulsive Esmeralda married in an access of misplaced pity. If ever anyone needs protecting from her own generous nature, Esmeralda does.'

Jane met his eyes levelly. 'You'll change your tune in a few months, Mr Adair. Everyone loves my mother. I'm not suggesting she's another Pollyanna, but she has a knack of bringing sunshine into everybody's life. Her only failure was with my grandfather, and he was one of those pots flawed in the making from the beginning. You'll see how my godmother will blossom. She already looks twice as well as when I first saw her, despite your care of her. Louise and Lauris are charmed to have a granny at last. They're high-spirited, like most eleven-year-olds, and get up to lots of mischief we could do without, but with old people or babies they're just sweet.

'Right this minute, because of your attitude, I'd like to stalk clean out of that door and go back to Oamaru, but when you're the breadwinner of a family newly-bereaved you can't do that. Oh, don't look so embarrassed . . . I'm not looking for sympathy, just stating that I can't afford a grand gesture like that. And apart from that, even now I'd never leave my Esmeralda. I just love her.'

46

His eyes narrowed. 'At the moment she looks like any-body's idea of a fairy godmother. She's hale and hearty, but she is, after all, eighty. How will you feel if she becomes a liability, if she's crippled with a stroke, or her heart ailment worsens? I don't want her let down again. And I warn you, if you have any thought of digging yourselves in here, and letting her go to a home if she fails, I'll have you out of Wedgwood House pronto. You're renting that only as long as Esmeralda lives.'

Jane turned white with suppressed passion. 'And what has it to do with you? I know you've known her most of your life, but you're not a relation. We may be only steps, but at least there's a connection. I find all this extremely strange—as if you had some ulterior motive.'

'I have a motive, admittedly, but not an ulterior one. If you must know what it has to do with me I'll tell you. I happen to be the——' He stopped, seemed to consider his next words. 'Well, let me put it this way. I'm in the nature of a trustee of Esmeralda's affairs. I've taken my father's place in this, and believe me, no one will ever take advantage of her.'

Jane picked up the basket. 'I see. Fair enough. But let me tell you, Esmeralda will only have good from this branch of the Grey family. I foresee that in less than a month, Mr Adair, you'll be eating your words, and though I can't see you admitting it, you'll be very glad we came to Wedgwood House!'

As she got to the door his voice arrested her. 'Esmeralda asked you to make it Rory. You'll have to do that so that she doesn't get upset at our attitudes towards each other. I must make it plain to you that you're to tell her nothing of this conversation. I will not have her upset.'

Jane's voice was like chips of ice, her eyes pure green. 'In that, at least, *Mr Adair*, we are at one. Neither will *I* have her upset. However, I don't think I could come at Rory; it doesn't suit you. It's a friendly sort of name. Now Broderic, I could. It's a stern, craggy sort of name. And by

47

the way, I'll show you the rent book every month—oh, yes, don't look surprised! I bought one in Oamaru. I've already given her the first instalment in advance.' Three steps further on she halted again and looked back over her shoulder. 'And there's something else. You're not the only one to lay down the law. I will not have my mother, my gallant little mother, or my sisters, feel unwelcome. If you do, I cannot undertake to hide from Esmeralda that as far as I'm concerned, you are the flaw in an otherwise perfect setting!'

She wouldn't even allow herself to slam the door.

CHAPTER THREE

DESPITE everything, Jane woke next morning to a sense of gladness and adventure; something to do with the sunlight peeping in on her, a bellbird chiming in what seemed perfect unison with the song of the Adair Water rippling over its shallow stony bed.

She went to her window, pulled back the curtains, heard the bird's song cease as though she'd disturbed it, but no, there it was, dipping its beak deep in one of the pendulous golden blooms of the *kowhai* that drooped above the water. She watched fascinated as the small, olive-green bird almost turned upside-down to insert its brush-like tongue in search of the honey it loved.

She heard a sound for all the world as if someone in taffeta approached, with a rustle of the stiff silk. A *tui* lighted on a flax-bush and it ceased. This indeed was Eden-like, no noise pollution here . . . in this peace one could even hear the winging of a bird! This one too foraged for sweetness in the depths of the dark-red flax-flowers. It too said its grace in song, but while most of its notes were almost the same as the *korimako*, the bellbird, it had a larger repertoire, with strange whistlings and chucklings, ending with a note of deep music as if it had twanged a woodland harp.

Its dark feathers glistened iridescently in the sun and the curled knot of feathers at its throat really was reminiscent of over-starched white bands . . . no wonder it was sometimes called the parson bird. Sparrows gathered hopefully on the branches of a maple that grew near a bird-table, and eyed its bare top reproachfully. Jane decided she'd better go and soak some crusts for them. She grabbed a wrap and peeped in at Esmeralda's room.

Esmeralda turned her head and smiled a smile of sheer happiness. She'd been lying looking out of her window. The sun glinted on the beautiful white hair and turned it to silver-gilt. Jane dropped a kiss on the pink cheek. 'I'll bring you breakfast in bed, love.'

'Just bring me a cup of tea now. I'll have my breakfast up with you, Jane. It's so lovely to have someone here and to know it will be that way till the end now, so I don't want to waste a moment lying in my lazy bed. When a body gets to my age, every moment is precious, and never more so than since you came to me.'

Jane said, 'I hope when I'm your age I'll have a zest for life like this. I'll run outside with bread for the sparrows while the kettle boils, and I'll run your bath while we have our cuppa.'

She sang as she spread the crumbs on the bird-table, Browning's *Pippa Passes*, the song of the little mill-girl who had only one day's holiday in the year . . .

> 'The year's at the spring;
> And day's at the morn;
> Morning's at seven;
> The hillside's dew-pearled;
> The lark's on the wing;
> The snail's on the thorn:
> God's in His heaven—
> All's right with the world!'

Jane's world *was* going to be all right, despite the distrust of that man at the homestead. She smiled to herself as she gazed about her. It seemed to her an omen of happiness that above her, soaring high above the Peaks of Starlight, a lark was singing, singing. On the rocks used as paving-stones about the bird-table, a snail had left a silver trail, and every hillside was, indeed, dew-pearled.

She ran in, her yellow cotton gown flowing out behind her. She cut wafer-thin brown bread-and-butter, put it on a willow-patterned plate, fitted a huge padded cosy over a blue speckled Moorcroft teapot and took the tray in.

Esmeralda's happiness was infectious. Jane's fears fled. They ate a hearty breakfast, washed up together, made their beds, wielded mops and dusters. Jane had refused to allow Esmeralda to show her their quarters last night lest she become overtired, but now they went on a tour of inspection.

Esmeralda's rooms all opened off the long corridor with the pot-plants. 'We shall call it the conservatory,' declared Jane, 'as if this were a stately home. Even the word conservatory has an elegant sound.' The rented part was through a locked door at the far end. 'We shan't need that key again,' said Jane. 'We're going to be a real family now. I've always thought that no family is a true one unless it has at least three generations. That's what I've got at last.'

The door opened into a barely-furnished living-room, but with their bits and pieces from Fiji, they'd soon make it homelike. 'And of course you'll be in watching TV with me at nights,' said Esmeralda, 'or playing Chinese Checkers or Monopoly, or just reading.'

The kitchen led off it and had been, when the building was a school, a morning-tea room for the staff. It was well equipped, even to a large fridge with a small deep-freeze compartment on top. A door led out to a laundry, and a shower-box. There was a separate bathroom nearer the four bedrooms which were off a corridor, and they had been classrooms. Esmeralda said, 'If you would use the bedroom you used last night, child, next to mine, that would give you and your mother a room each as a studio. The end ones, because those two have the best light.'

Jane continued to believe that this was a paradise. Esmeralda continued, opening doors, 'The bedrooms aren't the last word in luxury, but I did get good mattresses for the beds—I like people to sleep in comfort. The beds were discarded from Starlight when Rory's mother had the place redecorated, and they felt it saved me having to lay out too much money. What do you think?'

Jane hugged her. 'It's simply marvellous. We've all our own linen and blankets of course, and a few pieces of furniture Mother couldn't bear to part with; china, pictures galore, ornaments. And the matting. We'll have it sent here from Port Chalmers when it arrives by cargo boat from Auckland ... that is, Godmother, if you're quite, quite sure?'

Esmeralda swung round to face her. 'Jane! Night after night I've lain me down wondering if it might be my last spent among my loved mountains, my garden, my birds. Now I feel my future is here and will end here. There's to be no more talk of you taking from me, as you said in Oamaru. You're giving me something so much more precious than a roof over your heads ... you're giving me love and security and peace of mind. Now let's start redding this up and no nonsense about me helping. It'll be less tiring than gardening, and that's what I'll be doing if you turn me down.'

Jane assented. 'What hours do you open the shop, Godmother?'

'No particular hours. I'll show you later how we work it. Rory has a mechanical bent. He fixed up a sort of housephone. It's under the verandah of the shop with a notice saying lift the receiver, turn the handle, and say tourists have arrived. Then we go down. Sometimes it's prearranged. The bus depot or one of the guesthouses puts through calls to say they'll have a crowd here at an approximate time.'

Nothing was quite so enjoyable as creating a home, Jane thought. Esmeralda had to be restrained. Work came naturally to her. She must have been on good terms with it all her life.

Jane found a wheelbarrow and unpacked the caravan; she'd managed to bring a vast amount of stuff. It would save freight charges. The studio floor would have to be bare till the matting arrived, but she set up her sturdy easel, leaving the folding one in the van. Esmeralda told her to bring in a shabby kitchen table from the laundry for her paints and jars, and suggested she used a bookcase from the living-room for her books of paintings and photographic studies.

This room had an old-fashioned register fireplace that

threw out a great heat, she was told, and on it Jane stood her stepfather's photograph, her mother's, the twins'. Esmeralda brought in a black vase of white lilac that added an artistic touch to the bare surroundings.

Jane stepped back, viewed it, said, 'Ah ... Jane's herself again. The tools of her trade are to her hand ... there's beauty without and within. Oh, that flat drove me mad! The lack of space, the noise of the traffic. We were right on a bus-stop. In Fiji we had the soughing of the wind in the palms, the murmur of the sea. I can really paint here.'

She saw Esmeralda turn her head, turned her own to see Broderic Adair standing there. 'The main thing will be can you sell them here,' he said.

Jane took it calmly. 'I couldn't agree more, but nothing venture, nothing win. I expect all people who suddenly decide to live by their art, whatever it is, acting, painting, know a few tremors. But if they never dared, never staked faith in themselves against security ... and other people's doubts ... the world might have been a lot poorer. That may sound arrogant and it probably is, but any creative work takes faith, an arrogant faith in one's own ability. Dad believed he could make a better living here with palette and easel than in Fiji—he certainly painted better pictures —but death intervened. I'm convinced I'm meant to take on where he left off. I'm determined to make a go of it. But if it shouldn't turn out as profitable as my turnover in Queenstown and Wanaka led me to believe—well, I've earned my way waitressing before. Mother has this little Mini and I could travel in to Queenstown every day. But from what I sold last month, I made double what I could have earned at anything else. And that's the sort of money we need, so that in her later years my mother may know what it is to have her own rooftree.'

Esmeralda chuckled. 'You must join the Country Girls' Club. You've a turn for speeches. I'd like to see you debating against the Young Farmers' Club, especially against Rory. I don't recall ever seeing him at a loss for words before, and I'm naughty enough to enjoy it.'

Jane wished he had looked set back at this candid remark, but he put his head back and laughed. 'Let's say it's not so much searching for words, but waiting for a chance to applaud such rhetoric.'

Esmeralda heard her phone and went to answer it. Jane looked Broderic Adair straight in the eye and said, 'If that was to make me feel a little foolish because I defended my decision to launch out on my own, then you failed. I think I've got the ability to paint *and* the business acumen to make a go of it.'

The grooves in his cheeks deepened as he smiled. 'Jane, I think you have too. I rather think you've lots of spunk, and spunk is something I admire. But . . . protecting Esmeralda from herself is a deeply-ingrained habit of my family, and I'm the only one left here now to watch her interests. She gets caught up in other people's enthusiasm. Her heart rules her head. She's too old to be let down again. If this isn't a wildcat scheme, I'd be the first to praise your success.'

'That's really big of you,' she flashed, then subsided as Esmeralda came back.

Broderic Adair said, 'I'm going into Maunga-Whetu for some stores. Thought you might need to stock up yourself, Esmeralda, after a month away.'

'We do. Thanks. Jane, don't take off that becoming artist's smock. It's a good advert. People will expect you to dress like that.' It was floral, in a pattern splashed with anemones and marigolds, and she had a big black bow pinned at the neck. It had been bought solely with the idea of not showing paint smears. She said so now, pulling it out, and adding, 'More paint than design now, I'll peel it off and put a jacket on.'

She grabbed a fawn suede jacket from the back of her door, slipped it over her tan trews and cream polo-necked top, used a coral lipstick, smudged powder over a rather shiny nose, and emerged with her purse in one hand and a big shopping-basket in the other.

'I may not get everything in this. Will they give me a carton to get my groceries in?'

Broderic Adair said, 'They will—but isn't Esmeralda attending to the commissariat?'

'She is not. That's over to the Grey/Eastwood clan now. Don't bring the subject up, for goodness' sake, it took me half last night to convince my godmother. We're getting this at such a cheap rental and she confesses she's a bit tired of cooking, so she'll be eating with us. Cooking for five's not much different from cooking for four, and I'll send her breakfast in so that the twins don't get on her nerves with their pre-school hassling. After all, the benefits are so weighted on our side, Esmeralda's just got to concede something and learn that while it may be more blessed to give than to receive, it's also blessed to learn how to receive gracefully.'

She thought Broderic looked at her with respect—a change.

He grinned. 'Esmeralda, you may have met your match. All your life you've been the giver. Now you must learn to take.'

Esmeralda looked amazed. 'Broderic Adair! How *you* can say such a thing is beyond me! Why, but for you I'd not have——'

'Enough of that, Esmeralda. Here's your bag. I've not got all day. The car's at the front.'

He introduced her to the storekeeper, one Alun Hughes, as Esmeralda's goddaughter, come to live with her. It was easier than explaining the whole relationship. Jane had been living in Fiji for years but was now staying with Esmeralda, he said. Maybe he'd seen her exhibition of oils in the Mall a month ago? And her mother and sisters would be here soon.

Alun Hughes asked her if she was going to run an account. Jane looked horrified. 'No, cash. You see, we've never been what you might call well-off, and it's always been a case of what you haven't got money for, you do without.'

'Wish a few more worked on that principle. Mind you, farmers have to do it that way. Their money doesn't come in every week, but my bills from the merchants are monthly, so I do wish there were more like you.' He added quickly, 'Not that I've ever had to remind Adair of Starlight to settle up.'

It was a darling village. The contours were gentle, the road swung off the main road, took a dip, then widened into a big triangle of grass, neatly shaven, with flowering trees and seats dotted on it. The buildings, few in number, were set about it symmetrically. The church was of local stone, rough-hewn, painted white, with pale blue sills and leaded latticed windows. Its roof and miniature steeple were of grey Welsh slates. A small graveyard, well tended, merged into the pine wood on the rise behind it.

The garage didn't have the usual clutter of hideously derelict cars and farm machinery rusting in long grass outside it. That part had been screened off by a high wall of vibrapac blocks and the house beside it was surrounded by a beautiful garden. A combined Public Hall and Youth Centre stood beside the church and, though modern, was constructed in ranch style and blended well with the landscape. Huge Wellingtonia trees towered protectively above church and hall.

The store itself wasn't a conglomeration of goods. It had been an old building, and no doubt in its early days would have deserved the appellation of stocking everything from a needle to an anchor, and heaven help the one who had to find either; but it was now beautifully modernised and gleamed in new paint and freezing appliances. It was run almost like a mini-market, but had the personal service of an old-time country store, with no payout desk. The stone-floored verandah that protected the goods in the windows from too much sun, had been preserved; it still contained forms where old identities could sit and gossip, and the hitching-rails were intact. Sometimes, still, a horse would be seen tied up there. A clean horse-trough stood in the shade nearby.

Jane itched to paint it. Truly her lines had fallen among pleasant places. It only remains for me to prove to this Broderic Adair, she thought, that this is not a flash-in-the pan move, that we're not taking advantage of an old lady, that we're here to stay.

It was another couple of days before she discovered that hitherto, since his parents moved north, Rory had come down to Wedgwood House for his dinner every night. Lisel let the cat out of the bag.

Lisel was sweet, and exactly what you'd expect of an Austrian girl, with long fair hair braided round her head and eyes as blue as gentians. The house they lived in was less plain than some married couples' quarters tended to be. Lisel said, 'That was because of Rory. He's a wonderful boss. Hamish had one of the *whares* before he was married, but——'

Jane said, 'Warry? What is that?'

Lisel chuckled. 'Fancy me having to explain a Maori word to a born New Zealander! That is funny, but I like it. A hut. There are four or five of them up on the ridge behind those poplars—the shearing team uses them. Many single men prefer them. They live their own lives there, you understand. In Mrs Adair's time they would go to the homestead for meals, the single workers. The married couple who lived here then left about the time Hamish and I were to be married. He came to Innsbruck for the wedding, and to meet my people.

'When we got back these kind Adairs, prompted by Rory, had had this white house painted brown, and put up that little balcony under the eaves and constructed window-boxes there to hold the geraniums. And along the verandah at the bottom, the rows of antlers, so I would not feel there was nothing of Austria in this New Zealand. That was kind, *ja*?'

'Extremely kind,' agreed Jane. 'But I think, Lisel, they would be very glad to have a girl like you for the wife of Hamish; so domesticated, so happy in nature, good with animals, loving the mountains. Some wives would not like the isolation—I mean, if they came from the city. And you have added to the Austrian air, haven't you? The garden must be your creation. I saw you had a bed of anemones there, just dying off, and that scree bed looks as if it has alpine plants in it, though I've not gone up to it yet. Has it?'

'*Ja.* There are celmisias, the mountain daisies, kidney fern, and New Zealand edelweiss and little mountain violets and snowberries. I cannot seem to grow the mountain lilies here ... odd they should call them that when they are really giant ranunculi ... but I have some I am tending, in a pocket of shingle away up there.' She pointed. 'I have the New Zealand gentian, of course, and some little ground orchids, and I'm trying to cherish some from home. The purple dwarf soldanell, the yellow anemone, purple martagon, viscous and the long-spurred violet. It all had to be done, you understand, with the permission and the co—co—something from the right department so that I introduce nothing harmful.'

'Co-operation. Lisel, I think that's lovely, and how you get time for it, I just don't know. Yet you do a day or two at Starlight every week, and feed Rory too.'

Lisel laughed. 'I like the extra money. I like to have my very own so that if my people are ill and need me, I can fly home, or take the children to see them every five years or so. Of course, till now it was only lunch I gave Rory.'

Jane seized on that immediately. 'Till when? And who——?'

'Till Esmeralda had her month with you, Rory always had his evening meal with her. It kept her cooking. Old people tend to neglect to eat the right things. It helped Esmeralda in other ways too.'

'You mean he paid her for his dinners?'

Lisel hesitated. '*Nein.* At least—well, the vegetables

58

come from the farm, you see, the ones she does not grow herself. She does the salad vegetables which Rory and Hamish find too fiddling. And the herbs. They grow the ones that—how would you say it? That crop on a large dimension?'

'Large scale. Like potatoes and carrots and cabbages.'

Lisel nodded. 'The station has its own meat, of course, even to beef. So, for the meals, the—the fundamentals were home-grown. Esmeralda supplied the frills, as she calls them, the puddings and cakes.'

Jane regarded her shrewdly. 'So my coming has made more work for you, Lisel?'

Lisel looked embarrassed. 'A little. But not to think I mind. Rory is more patient than most bachelors with the children, though I'm sure he would like more peace at the day's end. But——'

Jane made up her mind. 'Lisel, I shall see him and say that things must be the same as before. We'll give him his dinners. And if, when Mother and the girls arrive, he wishes that, he and Esmeralda can have their dinners alone. We can send them in.'

She knew where Rory was working this morning and he was by himself, which was ideal. He'd come down, asked for some of Esmeralda's cookies for his mid-morning snack, with the confidence of a favourite grandson who won't be refused anything, and said he was off up the Adair Water to free a blockage. In the last fresh some boulders had tumbled down, but hadn't presented much of a problem till an elderberry bush had got washed away and jammed between them. Debris had so piled up, a dam had been created and water was spreading on to the hill paddock, and another heavy rain could cause erosion.

Jane felt apprehensive. She was never sure how he would view her suggestions. She mentally planned several gambits, but when she reached him, a little out of breath, and he heard her and turned, they all went out of her mind.

His dog jumped all over her. 'Down, Bluey!' said Broderic

Adair sharply. His gaze narrowed. 'Is anything wrong? With Esmeralda? Or in Oamaru?'

It was quite kindly, and steadied her. She shook her head. 'No, if I'm panting it's because of the climb. I'm out of condition. In Fiji we swim just about all the year and it keeps one fit. Now I'm settled I'll start tramping round here to keep in trim. I've been flat out painting, and standing at an easel for such long periods is practically sedentary.'

He nodded. 'And living life at Esmeralda's pace isn't as easy as you expected, is that it? If so, admit it now, rather than let Esmeralda get any more attached. This was what I was afraid of; your rash decision to cast in your lot with her was taken in the first flush of enthusiasm for discovering a half-pie relative with room to spare. It filled me with doubts. I was courageous enough to express those doubts and you thought me a curmudgeon ... now didn't you? Own up?'

She said coolly, 'I did. But——'

'But now you understand, so you've come up here to tell me out of earshot of Esmeralda that you don't think it will work.'

Fury rose up in Jane and mottled her cheeks with red. 'Broderic Adair! I've never known anyone so apt to put words in other people's mouths! Who do you think you are? Sir Omniscience or the Lord of the Isles? You've the makings of a first-class despot. Do you really want to know why I came up here? I discovered from Lisel—who by the way wasn't making a complaint—that you used to have your evening meal with Esmeralda, and that your motive was altruistic, because it kept Esmeralda cooking proper meals and gave you an excuse to supply her with meat and vegetables. I came up here thinking better of you than I've done till now.

'Lisel said you were extremely good with the children but she was sure you'd rather have a little peace at the day's end. I thought so too. It's one thing coping with one's own children then, and another having someone else's at table.

One's own you can hush down if need be. All this, I thought, Broderic Adair! I realised my coming had disrupted your ways far more than I'd guessed, and I even admired you for saying nothing to me about it. I expect you told Esmeralda not to mention it, either. I gave you credit for thinking I might find it a chore to have a man coming in at night for a meal, making extra work when I was trying to add to my stock of paintings. And I arrived to find you assuming I was ready to give up! I don't find Esmeralda's slower pace upsetting my metabolism. I just *love* her. I've been sticking too close to my easel, that's all. Same as authors, I suppose, stick too closely to their typewriters when the pressure's on. Oh, you make me so mad! You—Ohh!' She actually gritted her teeth at him.

He'd been leaning on his shovel, still towering above her on the rise, and now the eagle-like face so close to hers broke up into laughter—helpless laughter. It made Jane madder than ever. She turned to flee down hill, stood on a loose rock and fell headlong.

She heard the shovel clang against the boulders, and in a split second he had her on her feet and held her, steadying her against him. She put up her hands to his chest to push him off, humiliated, close to tears. His grip was vice-like, the dark face close to hers. 'No, steady on. You'll come another cropper if you don't watch out.'

The green eyes flashed. '*You* were the one to come a cropper, let me tell you. Not physically, but in wrong judgment. But are you apologising for it? No! Not you!'

He was still chuckling, and she hated him for it. It was galling to be in such a paddy and have him treat it as a joke.

He said, 'Hold on, Jane, be fair. I've not had a split second in which to apologise. And apologise I'm certainly aiming to do. But one moment you were gritting your teeth at me and the next I was picking you off the ground. Now, hold your wheesht and give me a chance. I, Broderic Torquil Adair, do humbly beg Jane Esmeralda Grey's pardon for so misjudging her and do solemnly swear from this time forth to stop suspecting her of rashness and instability. As witness my hand on this fourth of November, in the year of our Lord, one thousand, nine hundred and———'

He got no further; laughter just burst out of Jane and drowned his voice out. The sound of it reached right down the hillside, and gladdened old Esmeralda's heart. Nothing like laughter for cleansing animosity out of two people's minds and hearts.

Broderic Adair said, 'Thank heaven! I thought I'd really blotted my copybook this time, and if you told Esmeralda what I'd accused you of, she'd tear my liver out. Have you ever seen her get her dander up? No, of course not, because you're the apple of her eye. But when she does we all go for cover. It's like making hokey-pokey. You drop the baking-soda in and the golden syrup fizzes up all over the stove.

'Perhaps I've carried my concern for her to extremes. I was pretty young when her first husband died, but I remember him so vividly. I should do! He taught me to fish, to play cricket, and gave me my first stamp album, my first camera. He was a natural father, Tom Mayfield, but never had a child of his own. Then for Esmeralda to marry that— that———' he stopped, remembering he was speaking of Jane's grandfather.

Jane finished it for him, 'That indescribably mean, selfish, beastly, cruel old Henry Grey who whittled away everything Esmeralda's first husband had left her. Broderic, I don't wonder you were so antagonistic at first. We must have seemed just another lot of spongers.'

His grip had loosened but he still held her. The hazel eyes smiled into hers. For the first time she thought they were warm eyes, a curious mixture of brown and green, but not cold, not hard. He said inconsequentially, 'That's the first time you've said my name naturally. Before it's been with the air of one who does it against the grain to please Esmeralda. You much more enjoyed saying Broderic Adair, didn't you?'

She giggled. 'I did. It's such a forbidding combination. Tell me, is your second name really Torquil? I've never met anyone called that before. I like it.'

He nodded. 'I was named for Tom, Esmeralda's first husband. He was Torquil too, which is Thomas but in the Gaelic. He and my grandfather were like David and Jonathan. Well now, this business of the dinners. It's all right. I was beginning to feel, not long before you arrived, that she was finding them a bit much. So——'

Jane nodded. 'So you'd really rather have your dinners with Lisel. Though from now on I'll be cooking them. But they wouldn't be the same as your old-time dinners with Esmeralda, would they? So you'd rather leave things as they are?'

His lips twitched. Odd that she'd never noticed before what a well-cut mouth he had. He said, 'Jane Esmeralda, did you or didn't you, not five minutes ago, accuse me of putting words in your mouth? Now you're doing it to me. I'd much prefer to dine with you and Esmeralda. I think Hamish and Lisel ought to have their family to themselves for the evening meal. She does the men's lunches too, you know, though they live so near that they go home at night. It will suit me very well. And listen, seeing that you're now attending to the commissariat, we must put it on a business footing. I must pay my whack of the grocery bill. Groceries, like everything else, are suffering from inflation and I won't expect—— Oh lord, what have I done now?'

Jane said, 'Broderic Adair! You supply everything for the first course now. The desserts and cookies will be on me, or the deal's off.'

He considered that. 'Don't feel you have to offer that merely because I put you on the level of the sponging Henry when first we met. Now, Jane, don't get uptight with me again. If that was never in your mind, and you'd have offered it if neither of us had heard of Henry and it was just a reciprocal neighbourly service, I'll graciously accept.'

'It was. Rory, what about lunches?'

63

He shook his head. 'No, Hamish and I work together mostly and Lisel's easy-osy about a floating time midday. It wouldn't be fair to you. So often the coaches call in about noon at the centre on their way from Te Anau to a one o'clock meal at Queenstown. I do our breakfasts, of course.' He grinned. 'I don't reckon you noticed, but you actually said *Rory*.'

She smiled back. 'So I did. But I rather like Broderic.'

'Even if it's forbidding?'

'Don't push your luck. I might flare up again.'

'Well, as long as you don't tack that Adair on again I'll let you use it. I felt I was being reprimanded every time you said it. Like to stay while I finish this? I won't be much longer. It would give you a spell from your studio.'

She nodded and sat down on a huge embedded boulder. He dug out more shingle from the bed of the stream under the last boulder that blocked it, then he put the shovel under it and began to lever it up. She said hesitantly, 'Would my weight help?'

'It would. It's so nearly coming. But stand uphill from me in case it swings.' He rolled a boulder to divert the water on to the blockage and lend force, then returned to his leverage. He counted, and at his 'Three!' they both exerted extra pressure and away it went, bounding madly downhill. Bluey leapt madly in the air, barking approval, then the water poured down.

Jane looked at the dog and laughed. 'I feel that way too. How nice to be so uninhibited. It's quite an achievement. I can see there's more to mountain farming than lambing, mustering, and shearing. You must have endless trouble with this sort of thing.'

'We do,' he said. 'Culverts are the worst. We have several with small bridges over them, and we have to keep them clear. Blocked-up water can do a deal of damage and I hate the resultant mess.'

'I've noticed what a tidy farmer you are. I like that. I know it's not possible to keep a farm garden or yard like a city section, but your fences and sheds please me, and you keep the lawns and edges so trim. I saw you out till dusk the other night with the shears. I felt like offering to help, but didn't want you to think . . .'

'. . . To think you were sucking up to me, to put it crudely. Well, I'll take that offer up right now. The spring growth is at its height. But don't let it become a burden. You're doing plenty for Esmeralda, and it mustn't eat into your painting time. That's your livelihood the same as the farm schedule is mine. Do the edges in my garden when time permits. And thanks.'

Jane helped him gather up all the debris that had banked up round the blockage, and they dropped it into a convenient hollow out of sight. They rinsed their hands in the Adair Water, sweetly flowing now, dried them on Broderic's handkerchief, called Bluey and made their way downhill.

Broderic said, 'I'll tell Lisel while we're having lunch that I'm reverting to dinner at Esmeralda's.'

Jane felt much easier in her mind. She went in to poach eggs, happy despite soaked trews, a scratched forearm, and aching muscles. She was no longer a cuckoo-in-the-nest. She was earning her *kai*. Or at least, she was earning Broderic's approval by cooking his *kai* and trimming the edges of his lawns! She found it hard to keep her mind on her painting after lunch.

She felt the dinner must come up to standard; no quickly tossed-up snack. Lisel was a beautiful cook. Fortunately she had taken some meat out of the deep-freeze last night. It was a choice cut of beef that Otago people called trout-of-beef and North Islanders called point-of-blade. It was trout-shaped, would slice like corner-cut of topside, and had a deep pocket in it which you filled with stuffing, then roasted. Their landlady in Oamaru had shown Jane how to cook it.

Esmeralda had a lovely brown salver in oval shape, it would look well served on that, and she would flank it with roast potatoes delicately browned (she hoped), wedges of pumpkin, deep orange, and serve dark gravy and steamed yams with it. No horseradish sauce, that would take away the flavour of the stuffing. For some reason Jane wanted nothing even vaguely reminiscent of tropical cookery, so she wouldn't serve a flummery type of dessert.

If he was a stick-in-the-mud for the solid dishes of his pioneer ancestors, then he'd have them. Serve him right if, after a heavy dinner like that, she served up a genuine suet rolypoly; but better not, it might upset Esmeralda's digestion. She thought of a light steamed pudding her mother used to make. She'd do it right now, as it took only an hour and a half to steam and she could re-heat it just before the meal. They had a coachload of tourists coming up from Lake Manapouri at five, so she must be well ahead. Jane abandoned her easel. This would underline for Broderic the fact that she was an old-fashioned cook not relying on packet puddings, even if they were modern society's gift to rushed housewives!

She found it hard to realise how her mood had changed from that redhot one when she'd belted up the hillside to propose that he had his dinners at the Wedgwood House and discovered he was crediting her with welshing on her scheme. Now she was filled with hope that it would all work out, that enmity would die a natural death, and as she proved herself, Broderic Adair would make her mother and the children also welcome.

She worked swiftly and happily, then at four-thirty, confident that all was under control, she donned a tussore-coloured nylon smock patterned all over with little orange-centred daisies and leaves, pinned one of her huge floppy brown bows to the collar, brushed her short golden-brown hair till it shone, slipped a brown Alice-band about it, and went down with Esmeralda to the Centre.

It was a mini-bus, and smaller passenger-loads were always easier to handle. Esmeralda was in her element. She sold three sets of herb-pots filled with her home-grown products, several lavender and verbena bags, a couple of pomanders.

Two of the tourists were from Christchurch and were enchanted to buy a watercolour of Mother's each, one of the Worcester Street Bridge with its delicate old-fashioned wrought-iron lace sides, and one of Cathedral Square as it was when the traffic flowed through.

She must insist that Mother took a week or two up there to keep up with current changes, Jane thought. These she had done from snapshots of long ago. Nowadays the Square was even more charming, with a continental air, since it had been cobbled with soft pink tiles, and sauntering citizens could enjoy the precincts.

An American bought Jane's picture of the Edith Cavell Bridge at Arthur's Point, and a tall girl with dark brown hair and peaty brown-black eyes looked longingly as Jane packed it expertly between layers of polystyrene.

She turned to the rugged figure beside her, said, in a whisper that Jane just caught, 'Oh, Giles, I'd have loved that. That bridge holds such memories.'

Jane handed the picture to the customer, thanked her, turned to the others, said, 'I aim to do another picture of that. I think that of all the amazing autumn colours I saw when I was painting here last fall, they were most vivid at Arthur's Point. It wouldn't be exactly the same, but near. And if it wasn't just what you wanted you wouldn't have to take it. I thought it sounded as if you might live near here.'

They beamed. The man said, 'We do. I'm Giles Logie, and this is my wife, Lucinda. Esmeralda hasn't had time to introduce us. My aunt and her husband, Robert Adair, run the guest-house Drumlogie. We came along with the guests today. Robert is a sort of uncle—more a distant cousin—of Rory Adair's. It's one of those complicated things. Robert's side of the family emigrated to Nova Scotia first, the others to New Zealand. Then the Canadian lot were led in turn to Waipu in the North Island by the Reverend Norman McLeod. Robert eventually came down here and married my aunt, so Rory and Kate are sort of cousins of ours by marriage.'

Lucinda's eyes were slits of mirth. 'Now the poor girl's

really confused! Jane, you may have heard of Drumlogie. It's on the other side of Queenstown, towards Moonlight. It sits right on the footstool of Ben Logie. Esmeralda told us all about you on the phone. We're so thrilled for her—to have someone of her own, after all this time, is just marvellous.'

This was good hearing. How nice to meet someone so wholeheartedly glad for Esmeralda's sake! Jane's spirits soared even higher. Broderic came in, caught sight of the Logies and strolled over, kissed Lucinda, gripped Giles's hand. 'Good to see you. But where's the son and heir? Oh, too big a day for him, I suppose?'

They nodded. Giles said, 'Besides, I thought Lucinda could do with a full day off. Kenneth's a job on his own these days. He was born with an itch to be up and doing. Was walking at ten months, climbing at twelve, giving himself concussion and bruises and all sorts of things, and damaging our nervous systems to boot. Still, perhaps he'll make an Olympic champion. I quite appreciate having my wife to myself once in a blue moon. And with Stella and Kirsty dancing attendances on him all day today, he'll not even notice we've gone.'

Broderic said, 'Pity you'd not let us know you would be with this crowd, and you could have stayed to dinner and I'd have run you back afterwards.'

Jane hesitated, then plunged. She'd an idea he wasn't sure if her dinner would stretch to two extras or not. 'Broderic, if you'd like that, it so happens there's enough for five. I put in a huge roast of beef and I can easily add some extra tinned vegetables, and the pudding's not one you can make small. I was going to re-heat the other half some time. How about it?'

Giles didn't hesitate. 'Done. Stella will love bathing Kenny and telling him his story. Now, Lucinda, no objections. I'm all for it. Lovely end to a perfect day. I'll telephone Star.'

'Star?' asked Jane.

Giles grinned. 'I couldn't say my "L's" when I was small, so always called my aunt Star. It stuck. I'll just see everyone back on the bus. I gave them all the local history on the way down, and Ben—the driver—knows it backwards anyway if they think up any more questions. Hey, Esmeralda, you're having dinner-guests, us. Look hospitable.'

She looked more than that. She looked delighted.

CHAPTER FOUR

WHAT a happy evening the five of them had. It was the first time Jane had ever felt completely relaxed and, what was more, confident that their future here could be without tension. She and Broderic Adair were on a different footing now.

The stuffed trout-of-beef was juicy and delicious, the vegetables done to brown perfection, which was a miracle seeing that they'd been down at the stall so long, and she eked them out with processed ones and crisp rolls heated in the oven. Jane felt Broderic was now regarding her as an asset, not a liability. He was enjoying being able to entertain, even if it wasn't in his own house, without feeling it might be too much for Esmeralda.

Lucinda teased him. 'Last time we came to Starlight I had to do the cooking. Oh, fair enough, Rory, you and Giles and the men were away up the Bruach all day! Still, it's always nice to have a meal cooked for you. There's an air of surprise about not knowing what's on the menu.'

Esmeralda chuckled. 'There's also a surprise pudding. That's what it's called, Apple Surprise. Turn it out, Jane child.'

Jane slid it out of its enamel basin on to an old platter of Esmeralda's, a faded blue and white dish with a pattern of Asian pheasants and roses on it that would have fetched quite a price on the antique market. Ah, it was perfect, praise the saints. How humiliating if it hadn't been and she'd had to open a jar of fruit! It had a golden-brown base which now, of course, was the crown of it. She carried it in and put a gravy-boat of butterscotch sauce to add to it.

They looked impressed. 'That beats your instant puddings hollow,' said Broderic. 'Though I've found them very handy if I've had to cook for my men.'

Jane sliced it down into wedges. It was almost as light as

a sponge cake and was dotted with golden sultanas. Giles said, peering at it, 'You said *apple* surprise. Where's the apple?'

'That's the surprising bit,' said Esmeralda, giggling.

'You mean because it's not there? That's cheating.'

'It's there all right, Giles. That's what makes it a reduced-starch steamed pud. You simply cream butter and sugar, add a couple of eggs and beat, then your sifted flour and rising, and then grate two cooking apples into it, the sort that go mushy. You sprinkle the basin with brown sugar and butter and spice first. You can do it without, but it's nicer this way.'

Jane was amazed at the serenity that possessed her. There had been anxiety about money for so long, the urgent need for a home, the frightening decisions to take about whether they should try for run-of-the-mill jobs or launch out into the deep, trying to earn by their painting. Now it was coming right, and the resentment and suspicion Broderic Adair had shown her because of old Henry Grey had melted like snow in sunlight.

Everything was enhanced by Esmeralda's new content and the unsurpassed beauty of the surrounding mountains, the proximity of the lake and that scented colourful garden. It ought to bring out the best in their talent. Jane knew a sudden unbearable longing for Mother and Lauris and Louise to be already here. She was horrified when her vision suddenly glimmered with unshed tears, and she looked down quickly.

Broderic, who was next to her, leaned forward, and Jane gained control. The men washed up, waving aside all protests. Outside thrushes sang their mating songs, blackbirds clicketty-clicked, somewhere a cricket chirped, a happy, summer-heralding sound. Esmeralda and Lucinda were chatting, ensconced in deep chairs. Jane moved to the window, stood there holding back the purplish curtains, looking out on the lavender dusk. She didn't hear the men come in till they both crossed to see what held her attention.

She laughed. 'Nothing and everything. Just that soft light between the afterglow and the night. See, the mountains go almost purple against the paler sky. I've a special feeling for that one star that pricks out over Steeple Hill. I feel it belongs to me. Ridiculous really, when so many generations of people here must have known and loved it too. Did the Maoris of old trek through these passes? They did? Even knowing that gives one a great sense of stability, of continuity. Good to know that, in a world where all is change and restlessness.'

Giles said, 'But certain values don't change. Like your appreciation of that star, for instance, linking it with the past. I wish I had your gift, Jane. You can take these scenes and commit them to canvas, or whatever you paint on these days, and no matter what happens in the future, ours, or the future of generations to come, you've preserved that moment of time for posterity.

'People who have known these scenes will be able to look back at them in nostalgic memory, evoked by your pictures. Others who haven't known them will be able to imagine what it must have been like before the necessity to get from one place to another twice as fast as twenty years earlier pushed a road through a valley that till then had never known exhaust fumes or litter; what it was like when just a river wound lazily through before it had to be harnessed or flooded to provide power.'

Jane turned to look at him questioningly, and Giles grinned. 'Oh, Jane, I'm not a crank on the subject. I try to be objective, not an extremist. People need warmth in their houses, light to read by, power to cook with. A city in a power-cut is a cheerless place. Here we have open fireplaces and branches blown down in gales to keep us warm when power fails—and so much space, smoke doesn't become smog; but industry needs the power to keep the economy on an even keel, and opening up roads in our hinterland can also bring great joy to the elderly, lets them see scenery that hitherto was only the privilege of those young enough

72

to tramp our Fiordland valleys. I'm a conservationist, yes, to the extent of knowing that our greatest work is not to impede necessary progress, but to insist that all these schemes are put through with a minimum of damage to the beauty of our countryside, and to make sure if vast sums are spent to bring these schemes to fruition, a good proportion must also be laid out upon re-planting and restoring.'

Into the subsequent silence came the sound of clapping from Lucinda and Esmeralda. Giles laughed. 'Sorry, Jane. It sounded like something from Gladstone and Queen Victoria, didn't it? Am I right? Didn't she once tell him not to address her like a public meeting? You'll have to learn to divert Rory and myself from our pet topic.'

'I'd like fine to know how to do that myself,' said Lucinda saucily.

'But,' said Jane, 'it wasn't altogether like a public address. It gave me a sidelight on my work I've not thought about before. Sometimes I hate to part with my pictures. Authors, at least, always retain copies of their works. But what you said, Giles, makes me feel that if they're good enough, they may continue down through the years and record for other people the beauty I see here and enjoy in this day and age. Now, let's sit down and you can tell me if you want that picture of the bridge and poplars much as the one I sold today, or would you prefer it from some other angle? You said it had such memories—do you want a morning scene, or an afternoon one?'

Lucinda and Giles looked at each other and collapsed into laughter. Then Giles said, 'Oh, dear, I think you're imagining us wandering along that road, hand in hand, and me proposing to Lucinda. Nothing could be further from the truth!'

Jane turned a little pink. 'Oh, did I sound a romantic goose? But you did——'

'Yes, we did say it held tender memories. A case of looking back on a very turbulent past.' He chuckled, looked for permission to Lucinda, got it, continued: 'These folk know how stupid Lucinda and I were with each other at first. That had been some night. Lucinda's ex-fiancée had turned up at Drumlogie looking for her, and we took him back to his motel. Now Lucinda had the quaint idea I was the local Lothario——'

Lucinda broke in, 'I wasn't the only one to think that, and the way you went on that night did nothing to disabuse my mind of that idea. Giles, I've a feeling you're not going to tell this story accurately.'

'I'll do the telling just the same, woman. Jane, to give her a chance to feel less upset about the incredibly stupid Harvey turning up—any man's stupid who lets a girl like Lucinda get away from him—I didn't bring her straight home, I parked. She was most suspicious of my intentions and flew at me like a tiger-cat.'

Jane took a hasty look at Lucinda to see how she was taking this, and encountered Broderic's gaze; he was grinning at her reminiscently. She hastily averted her eyes. He might just as well have said, 'A tiger-cat like Jane,' but that situation had been different. Giles and Lucinda had been attracted.

Lucinda chuckled. 'When I think of what I told him, it's a wonder he ever risked marrying me. I said I'd no time for this permissive-age stuff, that even a moon rising over Wakatipu had no effect on me . . . and he squashed my high-and-mightiness by saying he thought I needed some brisk exercise after the shock of seeing Harvey again, and billing and cooing was the furthest thought from his mind.'

Giles managed to regain control of the conversation. 'And I told her she should never have been called Lucy, it was a name for a gentle little girl and she was about as gentle as an active volcano! But we called a truce, had a good walk, then on the way home, in the wee sma's, just past that bridge, the car died on me. I can tell you I was jolly glad we'd reached a sort of armed neutrality by then, or for sure she'd have smacked my face and rushed back to the tavern there. Some hound had siphoned it out while we'd walked round the waterfront! But by the time we'd got there, home to Drumlogie I mean, although some turbulent scenes still lay ahead, the three miles walking over rough roads had somehow laid the basis for some sort of kinship of spirit. So any angle will do us, Jane. We can't expect you to paint it by moonlight.'

Talk became general. Evidently Giles and Lucinda knew from Esmeralda where Jane fitted into the scheme of things, and about her mother and the girls coming soon. As Jane served coffee, Lucinda said, 'You must bring them over to Drumlogie. The school holidays will be on, and Mhairi and Fergus, my half-brother's children, are near their age.'

Broderic nodded, 'And you could bring them over here for a bit. It's your busiest season. Your brother and Kirsty are flat out at the restaurant then, and there's everything here to keep them happy, the pool, the swings, the gym-bars. It would make the twins feel at home. They could sleep up at Starlight, Kate should be home by then. When they arrive, Jane, I'll get some of the village youngsters to come up to play with them. They do anyway, to the pool. We have a roster of mothers to superintend at certain hours, it's too dangerous otherwise, so your mother needn't worry.'

Warmth flooded Jane's heart. All was going to be well. He even said, when the Logies were ready to go, 'Better come with me, Jane. If you talk to me on the way back, it'll stop me going to sleep at the wheel. Esmeralda wouldn't mind. You'll be all right till we get back, won't you? Or would you like to come too, Ess?'

She shook her head. 'No fear. I was hoping you'd take off soon, I want to watch the late film. Off you go.'

There was a full moon over the dog-leg lake, as it was called because of its angles. They came up from the foot, mile upon lovely mile. On the far side, etched darkly against the bluer sky, were the peaks of the Eyre Mountains; on a few of them was a silver glitter of frozen snow, still resisting the warmer days of approaching summer. Stars sequinned the sky, and here and there a solitary light gleamed, giving evidence of some remote sheep station, or shepherd's hut. Across the water were the jagged outlines of the Bayonet Peaks, above them the sharp outlines of the Remarkables.

Jane was in front with Broderic. That was Giles's doing. She'd said hesitantly as he held open the door for her, 'Don't you want the front seat so you can talk to Rory?'

Giles chuckled. 'I grant you he's a good conversationalist, but in the interests of safety I don't usually get a chance to put an arm round Lucinda on these romantic roads, so if he's not insulted, I prefer the back seat.'

Broderic chuckled. 'Could be I prefer it this way.'

It was nothing but badinage, Jane knew. Despite Giles's preoccupation with Lucinda, there was no lack of conversation. The amount of local information they all loved imparting showed how long years of living here had not dulled the edge of their appreciation. How strange that this road had been in existence only forty years or so, when you knew civilisation had reached the shores of the lakes more than a century ago. But the sheer heights that dropped down to the lake waters and below them had been a mighty barrier then. When you looked at the sheer solidity of the Devil's Staircase looming mockingly above the road as if to say, 'You've only chipped a little bit of me away,' you realised what a mighty task it had been, and how easy it must have seemed to let the steamers be the access way.

These heights still had to be reckoned with. The roadmen had to be at hand to clear the culverts of boulders when torrential rain streamed down these almost perpendicular surfaces and swept all before it on its headlong urgency towards the trough of the lake.

They came into Frankton to find the Motor Hotel there a blaze of lights, and music playing; ran along the residential shores of the lake, with here and there a glimpse of A-frame houses, looking like Swiss chalets, and opulent-looking new houses with patios and sun-decks for dreamy hours spent gazing over the great lake in all its moods; they didn't go into the town itself with its lilliput shops with their continental air that went back to the days of the cosmopolitan gold-diggers, and that sat smugly beneath the high-rise blocks of motels mainly confined to the rim of the town, against its hills.

They swept out on to the Gorge Road, that led to the Skippers' Canyon and across the Edith Cavell Bridge, with Jane pointing out the very spot where she'd stood to sketch it the previous autumn.

'My dad was with me then,' she said to Lucinda and Giles. 'My stepfather really, but my father in everything but fact. Noel was so gorgeous, and such a pal to me. We were so happy that day. It was while we were painting it that he made his mind up that this was the spot above all others where he wanted to settle. Mother was thrilled. She was happy enough in Fiji because wherever Dad was was home to her, but in her heart she often knew nostalgia for New Zealand. It was a terrible shock when he died so suddenly, but I'm finding compensation in knowing that we're doing what he planned for us as a family; and in finding my step-grandmother, I also found the ideal setting for us.'

It was Broderic who said, 'Is an old school really the ideal, Jane?'

Jane said soberly, 'It's a roof over our heads, and because Esmeralda is so sweet with Louise and Lauris and they call her Granny, we seem to be a family unit still, even if a dearly-loved member is absent. I feel Dad must know and be pleased. That may sound overly-sentimental, but——'

'But it's so true, Jane,' said Lucinda. 'You see, your story is similar to mine. I lost a loved stepfather too. Our little boy is named for him, and I'm always conscious in moments of decision, and I go by what I feel he would have advised, that in a very real way he still stands at my elbow. You can't fail to believe in immortality and the nearness of the other world when you have that experience. I've a twin

77

brother and sister, both married and in England. I felt very alone when I arrived here, but not for long. Giles hove on my horizon and dispelled all loneliness.'

Giles had a squeak of surprise in his voice. 'I hove on *your* horizon? Stick to the truth, lass. *You* hove on *mine*. Jane, she was trying to catch a hare she'd accidentally injured and stampeded my steers and cannoned into me.' His voice dropped the indignant tone and said, 'And despite that, it was the luckiest day of my life.'

Lucky Giles and Lucinda, Jane thought.

Lucinda said, 'Jane, no doubt you're still feeling strange, but you won't for long. The lake will cast its spell upon you and will never let you go.'

There was a smiling, reminiscent quality in her voice.

Jane said, 'I can see that happened to you ... or was it Giles who wouldn't let you go?'

'Oh, that too——'

Giles said, 'She hadn't a chance. She saw the moon at the full through our moongate and the legend came true.'

Lucinda burst out laughing. 'Jane, don't let this man of mine gull you into taking that for gospel! He and I were at outs for long enough, and he made up a lot of nonsense about the moongate his father built for his mother. He said that what you saw through its circle—in my case Walter Peak—remained for that person the one spot beloved over all. I was suspicious ... it sounded more like Kipling than a legend from the moongates of the mysterious East, as Giles said. He unblushingly replied that that was where Kipling got the line from during his years in the East. I looked it up, and Kipling was talking about his native Sussex. A born liar, my Giles.'

'But it came true, my gentle Lucy, didn't it? That's still your favourite view?'

'It is. Now change the subject. Jane'll think we're a pair of sentimental nits—we seem bent on telling her the full story of our courtship, and it's far from an orthodox one ... fought like cat and dog most of the time. Jane, you are the only person I've ever heard call Rory Broderic, and I like it, how come?'

Jane said drily, 'He informed me at our first meeting, when Esmeralda wanted me to use his Christian name right away, that he liked only intimates calling him Rory.'

Broderic Adair positively barked 'What?' Then he said reflectively, 'I think you're putting that very badly, Jane. It was something about was Rory short for Roderic; I said no, that was my father's name, that Broderic meant son of Roderic and I was Rory to my intimates. I didn't mean——'

'Well, I thought I was being warned off from being too familiar too soon. It doesn't matter now. And incidentally, why is Roderic shortened to Rory?'

He said, 'Because the Gaelic for Roderic is Ruairi.' He spelt it out.

Jane said thoughtfully, 'In spelling, if not in sound, it could be Maori.'

They came to the rustic gateway of Drumlogie, and swung round and up, completely round a shoulder of Ben Logie, to come out, surprisingly, on the far side of it, and look down on Queenstown, asparkle with lights, with the last gondola like a firefly, it seemed, descending on its cables from the Chalet on Bob's Peak to the wooded depths below.

'Odd to call them gondolas,' said Jane. 'I'd heard of them before Dad and I came, and as I'd never heard of such things except as cable-cars, I imagined in my ignorance that you had Venetian water-traffic on Lake Wakatipu.' They all burst out laughing. 'Just imagine the size of the poles on those waters. The lake over twelve hundred feet deep!'

Giles said, 'Let's not worry about the time. The moon's at the full. Let's go to Mother's night-garden and look through the moon-gate. We may never get so perfect a night again.'

They skirted the guesthouse, ablaze with lights, and took a path through a large-grove, Giles leading, holding Lucinda by the hand. Jane stumbled over a root, and Broderic took

79

her elbow. The moonlight, sifting in through the filigree of branches, made a tiled, shifting mosaic of light and dark on the path. Little creatures of the night scurried away at their approach. A bird gave a disturbed twitter and the rustle of its wings was a protest against humans who walked in their world by night.

They rounded a small conical hill, bare of anything save tussock, and came through a cleft in the hills to a ridge and presently were in the shadowy sweetness of a garden planted with herbs whose fragrance rose up to them as they crushed the odd sprig. They came round an immense crag and there before them was the moongate. They'd come on to it from the side, so what Jane saw was not Walter Peak, but the glimmering reach of the lake that stretched south towards Kingston . . . and Starlight Peaks.

She stopped dead, said, 'That *is* looking down towards Starlight, isn't it?'

Broderic said, 'Yes, it's lost in distance and darkness, but directly ahead of us. But what they want to show us is Walter Peak, *their* favourite view.'

'I'll settle for this,' said Jane softly.

They came dead centre, and framed in perfect symmetry was Walter Peak across the lake, classical, remote, sheer perfection. Even so Jane knew that far south, where even the moonlight couldn't show up the jagged peaks of Starlight, lay what for her would always be the one spot beloved over all.

She realised now why Giles had called it his mother's night-garden. Every flower blooming there was white so that it would show up on moonless nights.

Lucinda said, 'Giles's father, unlike the rest of the family who are great talkers, is rather an inarticulate man. But this was Angus Logie's way of showing his Marguerite how much he loved her. Masses of marguerites, of course, and white roses . . . see, they're just starting to bloom; white alyssum, snow-in-summer, native clematis, white violets and all our white alpine blooms. Some were growing at terrific heights. Angus climbed up to them and brought them down in his knapsack.'

They decided against going into the guesthouse. It was far too late, and the homeward miles lay before them. Jane was glad, and she said so to Broderic as they moved off. 'I like people. I'm used to meeting masses of them in the tourist hotels in Fiji, waiting at table, but this is so beautiful, the moongate, the garden, and the thought and labour behind its creation, that I didn't want anything to overlay it.'

She sensed him take a quick look at her. He said, 'I feel that way sometimes Sunday nights. In the tourist season, the holiday crowds drift in off launches and out of the camping grounds, just in casual attire. We put coffee and tea on for them in the Youth Centre, but sometimes, after a thought-provoking sermon, I'd sooner just walk home through the pine-wood and think about it rather than have it overlaid with small talk, swapping tales of the size of the land-locked salmon and the thrill of the jet-boating down the Kawarau Gorge. Yet it has its value, of course.'

Contentment seeped into Jane. He had lost his reserve with her. He was respecting her. What Lucinda and Giles had told her had given her fresh heart. If *they* could have had such a bad start and triumphed over it, then——suddenly Jane's thoughts halted in their racing. Oh, how stupid! No, what she was really thinking was that if the enmity those two had known could melt away, then perhaps in time Broderic would completely cease to resent their intrusion into his life.

They were past the Devil's Staircase now. Jane said, 'What a lovely couple! Lucky people.'

'They are now. Lucinda had a very unhappy time for a while. It's no secret, so this isn't gossip. She'd thought all her life, till she was twenty-five, that she was Kenneth Darling's daughter. He and her mother were missionaries and were drowned in a flood in India. Then she found out she was the offspring of a bigamous marriage. It wasn't easy to take. But Giles came into her life at the right time.'

'Thank you for telling me. It's so easy to look at an ideal couple and not dream they won through to that haven only after storms at sea.'

She knew there was a new rapport between herself and Broderic, but she was surprised when this man she'd found so formidable till now suddenly said, 'What about yourself, Jane? Do you really envy couples like that?'

She took her time over replying.

He said, 'Oh, sorry. That's too personal, isn't it? Especially from someone who's only just stopped treating you as a suspicious stranger.'

She said quickly, 'Oh, no, I didn't resent that. I was just trying to analyse how I do feel about that. Besides, Broderic, perhaps it was only natural for you to have doubts when you saw Esmeralda taken advantage of by my own grandfather. You're as protective about her as I am for Mother.'

He nodded. 'I've the impression you've taken on being the man of the family. Is your mother delicate?'

Jane chuckled. 'You're imagining her a clinging vine. She's anything but. Certainly she's dainty, like her watercolours, but there it stops. There's a toughness in Mother that's quite surprising. She had to be tough; she was only a girl when she was widowed the first time, and had years of trying to help that cantankerous old man who was my father's father, and to support herself and me.

'That old man had marred my father's young manhood years, undermining his son's confidence. He almost, but not quite, spoiled their married happiness. Mother had to be the stronger partner, and didn't know what it was to have a shoulder to lean on, but she made her husband happier than he'd ever been when single. Friends of hers told me this, not Mum.

'She was tremendously happy with Noel, but twelve years wasn't long enough to consolidate their financial position, so now, when she should be able to take life in more leisurely fashion, she's had to put her shoulder to the wheel again. So I don't have any dreams of marriage yet. I want to get Mother established in a home she can call her own, and get the girls educated. On a weekly wage starting from scratch, it would be well-nigh impossible, but now I'm filled with hope.'

Broderic said, 'I think you'll make the grade. It's a relief to know you're nothing like old Henry. When I asked you about envying married couples I was thinking partly of Kate, wondering if all girls do. The Logies will be here a lot and I wonder how Kate will react. My sister.'

'Do you want to tell me? But don't if you think Kate would resent it.'

'She'll probably tell you herself. Kate's a physiotherapist in Palmerston North; not too far from Wanganui for weekends with Mum and Dad and my sister Isabel. Kate is an A to Zedder. Know what I mean?'

Jane laughed. 'Noel used to call me one; meaning that whatever I did, I did with so much gusto I often came croppers. Does that fit Kate?'

'It does. She's an all-or-nothing person. Yet despite all her wild enthusiasms for helping people, lame dogs over stiles and hero-worshipping teachers and ministers and what-have-you, and espousing lost causes, she never fell in love in her life till about a year ago. She's thirty. He was a nice chap we all liked, and I feel they'd have been wed by now if he hadn't kept a promise he made to a widowed sister of his and taken her on a cruise in the Pacific.

'I thought that was just the quixotic type Kate would fall for, but that they'd be birds of a feather. Well, I've no doubt the trip helped the sister, but he must have got bowled over by the island moonlight or something—you'll have seen it happen time and again—and he really played it up. Got involved with a woman; Kate found out. She broke the engagement, only salvaging her pride by not telling him why. She simply told him she'd had long enough to consider and she'd decided she didn't think he was the type for a long-term husband.

'Anyway, she thinks a change of scene would do her good, so does Mother. She says Kate's lost all her spirit and just exists. She'd rather Kate went to another hospital, with lots of people about her, but Kate's set on coming home to keep house for me, so she arrives in December. She's used to all the fun and frolics of a large staff. I wondered if you'd work her down at the centre—at least she'd be meeting people, and not have too much solitude in which to brood. How about it?'

Jane's heart lifted. He was actually asking her aid. 'I think that's an excellent idea, Broderic. Don't be too obvious about it, I'll broach it. Say I'm at my wits' end trying to keep up the stock, look after Esmeralda and the shop. Will she be down before I get Mother and the children here?'

'Much about the same time if they're not coming till the primary schools break up for the summer holidays. That's the week before Christmas, isn't it?'

'Yes, but Mother thinks we ought to try to get settled before then so that we can be ready for the big influx of tourists. As soon as the girls get their exams over, she'd be ready to come.'

'Good. Can you manage my dinners till then?'

'Sure can. I'm thankful to be able to do that much, and I'd hate to feel Esmeralda didn't get as much of your companionship as she's been used to. You've been part of her life for decades, while I'm a newcomer. I know now how much Esmeralda owes to you, the meat, the potatoes, the firewood . . . you've made life possible for her these last few years. Oh, Broderic, I'm so glad we found her. I feel we can give her the family companionship she needs since she lost her first husband.'

To her great surprise his left hand came to pat hers as they lay on her lap. 'I'm glad too, Jane Esmeralda.'

She laughed lightly. 'No one's ever called me that before you did.'

'It suits you. I heard a Canadian woman the other day say

84

that even if she hadn't liked the picture subject she'd still have wanted it because it was all greens and golds and grey rocks and it was signed Esmeralda Grey ... "and that girl, the artist, is so exactly an Esmeralda Grey ... look at her, dear," I looked too and had to chuckle. You had on grey trews checked in green and that smock thing with the leaves. She sure thought she'd had her money's worth ... but aren't they funny?'

Jane laughed, a little self-consciously, 'I hope they don't think I dress up to my name. I naturally go to those colours because I love them. Perhaps I should get some reds and blues.'

'Rubbish. Anyone with eyes so green would dress up to them. Let it be.'

When they drew up outside Wedgwood House where Esmeralda's light was still on, Jane said, 'Now, don't get out. This is no hour for a hard-working farmer to get home.'

He said firmly, 'Of course I'll see you inside. Partly because I'm a chivalrous guy when I'm not surly like I was at first, and partly because I always like to satisfy myself that Esmeralda is okay. The times I've found her fallen asleep with the light on! I know you're here now, but I'm not sure you'd call me if she took some sudden turn. You're rather good at coping.'

What a warrior Esmeralda was! Even after the late film she was wide awake and reading. She looked like a naughty child, caught out. She giggled. 'This is the most fascinating mystery. Seven corpses! It's just littered with them, and I'm not halfway through. Yet it's such a nice book, nothing really morbid or violent about it. They were all either old or bad. That's the sort of whodunnit I like. And this gorgeous policeman is going to solve it. I can't stand smart-aleck investigators.'

Broderic said, 'What a naughty old lady you are! You ought to have hot milk and nutmeg at nine and off to sleep. You are just *not* finishing that book tonight. Give it here. No, Esmeralda, I don't want another cup of tea. You and

Jane both need your beauty sleep. While as for me, sleep will now knit up the ravelled sleave of care.'

'Have you a ravelled sleave of care, Rory?' asked Esmeralda.

He grinned at her over his shoulder as he shepherded Jane out. 'Not any more. I think Jane has taken a great load off my shoulders, you bad girl.'

'I'm glad you've at last realised that,' said Esmeralda, closing one eye in a wicked wink. 'Goodnight, children.'

'Come and lock the door after me, Jane. It's so easy to get careless in an isolated area like this. Time was when our doors were never locked, but it doesn't pay anywhere these days.' He hesitated, a hand on the doorknob, and said, 'Jane, isn't it a bit extreme?'

She blinked. 'What's extreme? Oh, you mean Esmeralda staying up so late at her age? Oh, we weren't here, so we couldn't do a thing about it. And what does it matter? I think the worst thing about being old would be getting hounded round by the young fry. I'm a great believer in letting people please themselves.'

He waved that aside, and laughed. 'Sorry, I reverted to an earlier topic. Odd, isn't it, how one expects people to be on the same wavelength? I mean about you regarding yourself as your mother's and sisters' mainstay. And saying that for you, for years anyway, marriage is out of the question?'

The green eyes looked steadfastly into the hazel ones. 'Please don't ever mention that to my mother, Broderic. She's the exact opposite of the possessive type, but I'm determined to be single-minded and heart-whole for a few years till I get them on their feet. Oh, I know it's easy to say, I've never been in love, but my aim is to get enough behind us for a substantial deposit on a house. I know now that it can be done.'

'Yes, I'd think so, the way you're going. But how satisfying is it emotionally?'

She stared. 'As satisfying as your own bachelor existence, I'd say. I'm hardly suffering frustration. There's not a male

86

on my horizon I'm even remotely interested in, and if any dawn I'll be careful not to lead them on.' Her tone was flippant. 'So your single workers are quite safe from me, Broderic Torquil Adair!'

'That's far too nun-like an existence for anyone as vital as you. Don't you ever want to go to theatres, parties, dances?'

She shrugged. 'Oh, I expect I will some time, when I get settled. I had quite a gay time in Fiji, you know, especially when I was waitressing. We were fair game for all the un-attached tourists. They often wanted a partner for going watching the fire-walking, barbecues on the beaches, moon-light bathing parties, but I never got serious about any of them. Well, if I suddenly get an irresistible yen to dance the tango—or is Scottish country dancing the in-thing here?—I'll call on you to squire me. Seeing you know I've no serious designs on any male, I couldn't be accused of leading you on, could I? We could partner each other to certain events without feelings involved on either side. And now, out! Do you know it's two-thirty?'

He gave her a strange look, turned the handle, and said, 'So I suppose *au revoir* would meet the bill better than goodnight. Sleep well, Jane Esmeralda.'

CHAPTER FIVE

From that night on Jane was conscious of a quite different relationship between herself and Broderic Adair. They were now partners, united in their devotion to Esmeralda, and Jane was sure that he was appreciating the fact that his reponsibility was less. Mick and Bernie, his two men, said so to her. Lisel had taken Esmeralda into Queenstown and Broderic was at a sale in Lumsden, so Jane had cooked lunch for the men.

Bernie gave a guffaw. 'You should have heard him, Jane, the morning after you arrived. His idea of an artist was of someone dreamy, head-in-the-clouds, someone who wouldn't knuckle down to housework and dishes. You know, all soul and no gumption. You remember I was with him the day we came down and found you up the manhole in the ceiling cleaning out the bird-nests? Rory's face was a study. Even Lisel wouldn't take on that job. And when he found you were keeping the kindling boxes full and cleaning the fowls' dropboards, he had to admit you were a bit of all right.'

Yes, Jane knew she was one of the gang now, and it added variety to her day, giving her a change from painting and selling, sometimes to take the flasks and sandwiches up to where the men where working, to be called on once in a while to assist them yarding sheep and lambs. It was not only novel to her, but the mere fact of turning her hand to these things gave added power and understanding to her sketching pencil. They laughed at her when they found that even on those jobs she carried a small sketchbook in her back pocket, but they were interested enough to ask her to explain when she said it gave her something.

She said, 'Well, it used to puzzle me how some of the world's greatest artists had come from the peasant class. Then I realised that they had been so close to the elemental things of life that they portrayed them with accuracy and understanding. When they sketched in the tired lines on a woman's face, they remembered how they, in childhood, had had to help carry heavy baskets of washing to the streams; when they beaded sweat on a labourer's brow, they recalled long hours of drudgery in the fields, under the hot Italian sun; when they sketched in hollow cheeks and gaunt framework, they remembered there wasn't always enough food to fill their stomachs.

'And so with me. I don't want to paint just mountains and trees and lakes. I want sheep-yards, and men with aching backs after the dipping, and I can get the droop of the shoulders and the dust-shadowed eyes better if I've known just that myself.'

Mick said, 'Well, I'm beggared! You'll have me taking up painting next. I hadn't realised there was so much in it.'

She took on the grooming of the donkeys. Minto and Pinto loved this and it became a familiar sight to see Jane going through the paddocks with two eager donkeys trotting along behind her, nudging her. 'It'll run some of the fat off them,' said Broderic, 'but when the girls arrive they'll get more exercise. Since Josef and Gretchen got their ponies, the donkeys get the go-by.' Jane could hardly credit how different he was. She had proved her worth and was now accepted as one of the workers on the estate, while still spending most of her time at her easel, or off on scene-hunting forays with Esmeralda beside her. There was no end to the variety. There were old stone bridges, goldminers' huts, most of them suffering from Anno Domini in the most paintable way, creeks that tumbled through clefts in the mountain ways, winding roads leading into sunlit copses, strange, endearing formations of rocks and bluffs.

She loved painting gum-trees with their glorious multi-coloured trunks and peeling bark, and the fan-clusters of cabbage-tree tops, patterning cultivated hillsides with a symmetry of design.

By now Jane had done a whole series of paintings of the

various features of Esmeralda's hillside garden, the drystone walls, the tables she had contrived out of the same material with an artistry that made you wonder if it had been inherited from some Cotswold ancestors of long ago; her wandering paths of stones set in turf, testimonial to hours of hard labour; paintings of her trellised arches, hung with plumy wistaria or smothered with the tiny cream rosettes of banksia roses; the sundial, set in a base of the multi-coloured rocks from the Shotover River, lavender, rose, slate-blue green, and the startling white of country quartz, that looked as if it ought to be gold-bearing but wasn't.

When she had finished that set to her satisfaction, she took advantage of Esmeralda being busy in the shed that housed her kiln, to hang them on the back of the conservatory. When Esmeralda discovered them she was enchanted as she walked along, examining each with delight. 'But, Jane, hadn't you intended these for the shop? People who already have a lot of mountain pictures or autumn scenes might easily want these more intimate garden corners.'

Jane shook her head most decidedly. 'No, Godmother. They're my small thank-you for giving me this chance to keep my family by doing the thing I love most to do. I wanted what I gave you to be a little bit of myself.' Neither of them had noticed Broderic come in.

A tear of pure joy rolled down Esmeralda's pink cheek. 'That's perfect, Jane. I accept gladly. This means more to me than anything else could. It reminds me of something Emerson said, and my own mother was very fond of repeating it. She liked the presents we made her ourselves, clumsy little things for the most part. I can hear her now: "Our tokens of love are for the most part barbarous, cold and lifeless because they do not represent our life. The only gift is a portion of thyself, therefore let the farmer give his corn; the miner a gem; the painter his picture; and the poet his poem." '

The sound of clapping behind them made them both swing round to see Broderic grinning. 'Bravo, Esmeralda, for that. Jane, do you think either of us will have a memory like that in fifty years' time?'

Esmeralda looked sober. 'When one is old, lad, one remembers the things learned in childhood, but forgets what happened last month, last week.'

When Broderic smiled like that at Esmeralda Jane wondered how she could ever have thought him forbidding. He said, 'When what you learned in childhood, Esmeralda, is as lovely as that, I don't think more recent things matter.' He added in mock rue, 'I'm almost jealous. I don't remember you quoting things like that about me.'

She took him seriously. 'I mayn't have quoted them. I did think them.'

He looked alarmed. 'I've a feeling you're going to take a dirty crack at me, not pay me a tribute. To take me down a peg!'

'No, not this time. It was when you allowed the new road to go through your land at great inconvenience to yourself.'

He looked embarrassed. 'Oh, come, Esmeralda, there's not much choice when road-building's on the drawing-board—or dam-building either. Cut out the bouquets.'

'I will not. I mightn't be here much longer to hand them out. You know as well as I do that there *was* a choice. They could have gone through Eyrewell's property. That was the first plan, but you thought he'd suffer more and was so newly established that it would affect him more than you. So you offered this. It reminded me of another American writer, I don't suppose anyone of your generation reads him—one David Grayson. I'm a bit vague on what occasioned the comment. I think it was some community project that needed financial support, and this man had given up his treasured dream of buying a piano to contribute towards it. David Grayson said that was true politics . . . the voluntary surrender of a private good for the good of the community. That's what that gesture of yours meant to me.' She turned to Jane. 'It cut off fifty acres. They're beyond the Stumbling Block Bluff. It cost him hours and hours of man-power moving his stock, to say nothing of extra fencing.'

'Well,' said Broderic, 'I hope Jane is now suitably impressed with the nobility of my make-up ... as I am with hers ... and to get back on to a less exalted basis, I came in to see if Jane could manage to mend the strap on this bridle for me. Will your old machine still cope with tough leather, Ess?'

The chores of the day were over, the shop closed, the meal served, the dishes washed, and a sunset in colours beyond belief was lingering above the Eyre Mountains. Down here in the south they had the long twilight of the Highlands of Scotland, lengthened now by an extra hour of daylight saving.

Jane was wearing purple trews with a lilac top patterned in green and black, and she'd tied the goldy-brown hair, a little longer now, back behind her ears with a strip of green gauze that floated out in two ends; because it had been stiflingly hot today, here in this wide cleft between the ranges.

She was standing at the conservatory windows watching the sunset lights change from fire to gold, from coral to burnt orange, behind clouds rimmed with silver and purple and a bright, unearthly green.

Broderic came through. She turned, said, 'Rory, where is that sheared-off bit of your land?'

'It's due south—over to the left, past the Stumbling Block. You can't see it from here. How would you like to come up Cruachan with me? It's a grand night for a climb. You get a great view from there.'

'Cruachan? I know Bruach is the steep bank above the Adair Water, but Cruachan I don't know. What does it mean, and where is it?'

'You can only see it from the back of the house. It's Cruachan Beann in full, and it means a haunch of peaks. It runs out, looking exactly like a deer haunch, from Starlight Peaks, below the Steeple.'

'Oh, I know it. I took it for a shoulder of the Peaks. I'd love to.'

He looked down at her feet. 'Better change those scuffs for something more substantial.'

She nodded. 'These were cool for cooking in. I'll put brogues on.'

He always changed from his farm-things for the evening meal. Tonight he was in walk-shorts in a cream and brown check, knee-length walk-socks and a dark brown T-shirt. His tan was a coppery one and his hair glistened like burnished bronze in the light from the sunset as he led the way, putting back a hand for her now and then.

Minto and Pinto looked up hopefully from their grazing as they entered the paddock and trotted after them. 'Not tonight, mokes,' said Rory firmly, closing the far gate between them, 'you're so crazy on nuzzling Jane you'd push us over the edge.'

They came up to the hip of the haunch, crossed it and went down the little dip on the far side that looked south-west. A gnarled old *ngaio* tree had miraculously rooted and grown among the rocks here, surviving who knew how many thousands of howling sou'-westerlies by leaning away from them. They went round the far side of it, in a world of their own, perched high above all of the Starlight Estate save the Peaks above them. Broderic pointed out his paddocks beyond the bend of the road. They were rich and green, dotted with sheep and cattle.

Jane turned to him. 'Broderic, I liked what my godmother said in tribute to you this morning. It means you're the sort of man to cast a vote for something that would benefit other people, even if it meant hardship to yourself. Oh, how I like it!' Her eyes were a-sparkle, her lips curved at the corners in a smile. 'This means you have to take your stock out on the road well north of the Crafts Centre, because you can't take them through Esmeralda's garden, and go right past it south to there. The Stumbling Block is well named, isn't it?'

He grinned. 'You ought to read how William Gilbert Rees brought his sheep up here in the old days, Jane. There were no roads, no bridges. Sometimes the scrub and pig-fern was so tight that they had to use fifty or so sheep as a spear-head, treading a way through, then spelling them to the back of the flock when they got too tired. Droving a flock along a couple of miles of highway can't be compared with that.'

A line appeared between her brows. 'H'mm. I'm not sure that's a good comparison. He was a pioneer taking up a tract of new country. This cut into an established sheep-run. But I also like the way you're playing down what you did.'

A smile lifted the corners of his mouth, a gleam appeared in his eyes. 'There are things about you I like too ... for instance the line of your chin and the colour of your eyes, Esmeralda. You ought never to have been called anything else.'

Jane, caught unawares by this sudden change from the general topic to the personal, blinked at him.

Adair of Starlight had had his hand resting on a branch of the *ngaio* just behind her. Now he brought it down to her shoulder, and his other hand turned her round to face him. 'And I'd not noticed, till I saw you in this light, that your brows and lashes aren't dark after all, they're the same goldeny-brown as your hair. So I very much like the full combination ... No, don't wriggle away. You're going to be kissed, Esmeralda!'

Kissed, she was, and very thoroughly. His lips at first were cool, and hard, then warm, demanding. Jane was aware as he ended that kiss of feminine feelings, only guessed at till now, stirring within her. He still held her, looking down and smiling. She couldn't quite hold his look or return the smile, and suddenly, to her chagrin, hot colour flooded her face.

He gave a shout of laughter, not derisive laughter, but tender. 'Why, Jane, you're so cool, so self-possessed most of the time, I never thought to see you blush. *Why* are you blushing?'

She looked across. 'I've no idea. What a question to ask!'

He went on laughing. 'Really, Jane, you're a constant wonder and delight. You keep on turning all my ideas of you upside down. I was sure you were going to be a liability, that Esmeralda was going to make another mistake and saddle herself with an improvident family ... and you've taken on more than I'd dreamed anyone could, *and* produce paintings. I reckon you must be half a stone lighter than when you first came. Slow down, girl, you've made your point. You're the best thing that's happened to Esmeralda in years ... come to that, the best thing that's happened to Starlight. Don't overdo. Relax. And ... keep on blushing now and then. I rather like it, I find.'

Jane felt waves of feeling washing over her and she couldn't analyse any of them. It must be relief. Relief that there was no antagonism for Mother and the girls to face. But now, at that last remark, she looked puzzled. 'You *like* me blushing! I *hate* blushing. It makes one feel gauche ... and very young. I'm not particularly young. I'm twenty-four.'

'A nice mature age. And you aren't gauche, ever, Jane. Even the carriage of your head as you walk denotes a certain confidence. That's why I like the blush!'

'You've lost me, Broderic Adair.'

He laughed teasingly. 'It's probably primitive. I think every man likes to think he can make a woman feel a little unsure of herself once in a while.'

'You mean the dominant male ego?' Jane was herself again, almost.

'I expect I do. Anyway, did you like it?'

'Like what?'

'Like being put in a flutter?'

For one moment her eyes flashed and he knew it, stepping back and putting up a hand as if to shield himself, then laughter bubbled up in her.

He said, mock-relieved, 'That's better. I thought I was going to have my face slapped. Oh, look, the sun is dipping down behind the mountains at last.'

They looked right into the fiery half-circle for one blinding instant, then it was gone with a last fling of dazzling colours raying up, pure marigold, tangerine, flame, coral, and amber. Then dusk softened every cloud with indigo.

'Come on, purple girl on a purple mountain,' said Broderic, 'let's go down, partner.'

Jane turned her face towards him as he took her hand to turn her about. 'Now that's something I like,' she said serenely, 'being called partner. It has a matey ring about it. Though when I come to think of it, partner in what?'

He began to say something, thought better of it, looked away, then back, and easily, 'Partner in the Protecting-Esmeralda-Concern, of course. What else?'

They dawdled down, stopping now and then to sweep the scenes around and below them with appreciative eyes; the spinneys of trees, the meanderings of the Adair Water, the winging home of countless birds from their daytime forage, the strange formations of rock, the jagged rim of mountains westward against the lingering afterglow, looking as flat as cardboard cut-outs on a nursery frieze, because the deepening night had blotted out their depth and contours, leaving only the tops silhouetted.

She said so, and he nodded. 'Oddly enough we've got just that around our old playroom walls on one side. Mother got us doing it once when Isabel and Kate and I were convalescing after measles. I've no artistic leanings whatever, but I made a better job of it than expected because I loved those mountains so much. As I should, seeing they're bound up with my earliest memories.'

'That must benefit a child greatly, to have such stability in his background.'

He didn't reply at once, then said, 'Yes, I was lucky. But on the other hand one is apt to be a bit set in one's ways, not so adaptable or tolerant.'

He answered the question in her eyes. 'I'm thinking of the way I regarded you with suspicion. Just because you'd moved about a bit, I almost dubbed you a vagrant, which was insufferable of me. We're all products of our environment to a degree, yet you had a strength of character that triumphed over yours. Jane, Esmeralda will be all right—she has three favourite programmes in succession tonight. You've not seen the old playroom, have you? Or even much of the house. What better time than now?'

This was a very different Adair of Starlight! He took her up the stairs first. It was all quite charming, rooms set in the deep roof with dormer windows, and the resultant nooks and crannies gave great individuality, allowing for fitted dressing-tables, and bookcases and window-seats.

The master-bedroom had a dormer back and front, and wide modern windows in the gable-end. Broderic said lightly, 'I suppose this will be the room I'll occupy when I marry, instead of that untidy one next door. It has this, just off it,' he swung open a small door and displayed a room with a paper that had teddy-bears and robins all over it. There was a spotless white table with a baby-bath on it, turned upside down, and an old-fashioned china soap-dish from a washstand set.

Jane took a look at his six-foot-two of solid muscle and bone and said, laughing, 'Tell me, were you ever really bathed in that?'

He chuckled. 'Sorry to disappoint you, no. That's a plastic one Isabel used for her babies when they holidayed down here. Ours is that chipped blue enamel one the donkeys get their mash from.'

There was a cot, a small bed, and a big box of toys, very battered. 'Those were ours. This was the one I took to bed, I called it Mac Adair.' He picked out a shabby blue velvet Scots terrier with a tartan collar. Jane ran her hand over it, and knew she'd never be able to think of Broderic as formidable again. She replaced it carefully.

They came down. The playroom was at the back, off the

kitchen, 'Where Mother could keep an eye on us on wet days.'

It had a row of windows that opened on to a stone-floored verandah. Two walls had friezes of Mother Goose characters, the other was pasted with Broderic's purple mountains. Beneath were blackboards, pegboard strips to pin things on, hooks for small raincoats and windcheaters, and a shelf held a row of graded gumboots. There were prams, dolls' beds, railway lines, engines, a rocking-horse.

'I leave these here,' said Broderic. 'Lisel brings the kids here on wet days and gives my house an extra redd-up then. The one they have is rather too small for much romping. When Isabel's children come they have a wonderful time, but they're not coming this January. They're going up to their father's people in Bay of Islands. By the way,' he added, 'Kate'll be here about mid-December. Her ex-fiancé has been relieving in someone else's territory—he's a traveller—but she's heard he's due back soon, so she's going to take off. Poor Kate! She still carries a torch for him.'

'Perhaps Mick or Bernie will take her mind off him?'

'I hardly think so, Jane. They're a bit young for her. She can remember them in the Primers when she was in the Standards—pity. Perhaps I should look round for an extra man, older.'

They heard footsteps, Bernie's. He was sleeping up in one of the *whares* because his mother had a houseful of visitors. 'Oh, there you are. I saw the lights on. Esmeralda thought you were away up Cruachan Beann, so I went as far as the new gate and hollered. Hugh Eyrewell's over at Hamish's and wanted to see you. Will you come over, or shall I send him here?'

'Ask him and Hamish to come,' said Broderic. 'I expect Lisel will want to see that Tyrolean programme and will be too polite to say so to Hugh. Jane, how about staying on to make us some coffee?—Esmeralda gave me a fair slab of your galaxy cake and ginger biscuits this morning. Ring Hamish from here, Bernie, and stay and have some with us.'

Jane went out to the kitchen. Broderic drew the lounge drapes and said to Bernie, 'Is it about the plans for re-modelling the church vestry?'

Bernie nodded.

'Then we'll sit up to the table and spread them out.'

Jane said, 'May Bernie and I have ours in the kitchen? You'd get on better without us, anyway, and he was telling me about an idea he's got for a mural for the Youth Centre for the New Year's Night dance.'

Bernie's ideas were good, Jane caught on. She'd love to do something for free for this community where she had been made so welcome. They got on with it.

Jane was conscious of a quiet happiness. The future looked more rosy. It mightn't be just one long grind of steady work in order to provide some sort of security for the family. She might be able to live some sort of a life of her own, such as other girls could look forward to . . . She pulled up her racing thoughts . . . really, how idiotic could one get in one's dreams? She said, 'Bernie, I hadn't realised till to-day when Esmeralda mentioned it that Rory had really made a terrific sacrifice to save Eyrewell's property being carved up. That he thought the older estate should bear the brunt.'

'Yep. My father thought that was big of Rory. Eyrewell's a good community man, and Dad thought he might get dis-couraged and take up land elsewhere. It makes a hell of a lot of extra work for this place, though. There are times when I curse it myself, but I've never heard the boss utter as much as a yowl. And who knows, it might be another decade before he can cut through and have access again.'

Jane looked startled. 'I didn't know there was any chance of that. I mean, a road is so permanent a feature. How come?'

'Oh, there's an agreement clause. The old school will come down when Esmeralda no longer needs it, and we'll cut a stock road through. It'll be costly even so, but it would be saved over a few years. Nobody will want an old school, of course!' He stopped, said, 'You're only living there as a stop-gap, aren't you? The boss said something when you first arrived about it. That even if he didn't approve of Esmeralda renting it out to you'—he grinned—'it was just to tide you over till you found a place of your own. In any case, if Esmeralda happened to check out this side of ninety, Rory'd do the decent thing, I know, and give you plenty of time to get somewhere else. I daresay you'll find it better in the long run to be nearer Queenstown, anyway.'

Bernie gathered up his sketches and said, 'Well, I reckon this'll go over well at the dance. Shows how good it is to have an artist right on the spot. Now, I'll go up to the *whare* and write a letter to my girl-friend in Roxburgh, so I can get it in the mailbox tomorrow morning,' and off he went, whistling, quite unaware that he had left Jane feeling shattered.

She sat on, doodling unseeingly on her pad, trying to take it in. She must look at it objectively, not as affecting herself. This had been arranged long before she herself had come into it. Vague remembrance of snippets of conversations kept coming back to her . . . that the land the school had been upon had belonged to Starlight originally; the first Adair had deeded it to the community. Esmeralda had once mentioned that Rory had had the chance of buying it back when the Starlight school was amalgamated with the others, but as her need was greater than his, he'd allowed her to have the school to live in. She guessed he could easily have outbid Esmeralda. There must have been some agreement then, that upon her death he was to have an option on the land. No wonder he hadn't wanted another family digging themselves in!

Esmeralda was over four-score years. At the thought, Jane knew a pang that was almost a physical one—not because they wouldn't be able to stay here, but at the thought of losing her godmother. She pulled herself together; Esmeralda would probably make a spry nonagenarian. The twins might have their 'granny' that long.

Jane walked along the hall and on to the patio to look down on Wedgwood House, where Esmeralda's light glowed behind the drawn curtains. The scents of this old garden rose up to her, roses, honeysuckle, lavender, mock orange-blossom ... it was almost impossible to imagine that school ever being razed to the ground and a roughly-metalled stock road pushed through it. It would seem to blot out Esmeralda's memory. What a pity the main road had ever had its course changed. None of this need have happened then.

A comforting thought struck Jane. Would a man who had planted a sapling by the edge of a lake miles from here, to replace one an old lady had loved, ever be able to bring himself to destroy all this beauty created by her?

She heard a door open and Broderic's voice call, 'Don't go yet, Jane, the others are just going. I'll walk you down the hill. It's rough going.'

Yes, she would wait. It would be a good opportunity to ask him about it.

Rory took her elbow. He seemed content to walk in silence, and Jane wouldn't break it. Sometimes silence was more intimate than words. It would seem self-seeking to bring up that topic now. Later, much later, she was going to wish she'd done just that, there and then.

They came down the rock steps to the squared-off ones set like flagging against the back door. Little aromatic plants grew in the crevices. Rory said, 'I won't come in, I can see she's still watching her programme. I used to drop in every night, the evenings I didn't spend with her, I mean, before I went to bed, but now I know she's in safe hands and happy.'

So Jane said quickly, 'You think she's looking well, don't you? I know she's eighty, but oh, I'd like her to have a few years as the pivot of a family before she leaves us.'

He looked at her sharply. The light Esmeralda had

switched on for Jane at the back door, was shining directly on her. 'Why, Jane, you suddenly look rather drawn ... why? Oh, I know, you haven't known Esmeralda as long as I have, yet you already feel something very good will have gone out of life when she's no longer with us. Though it seems you're less selfish than I am about that ... you want to give her longer of family happiness. Well, none of us can choose the time or the manner of our passing, but even if Esmeralda should die tonight, Jane, you've made her last weeks full of joy. Having another woman, even if in the granddaughter age, must make her feel secure. I've been near, but there are things a man can't do for old age. But you could, and would.'

He paused, added, 'So you're not to worry, not to feel insecure for yourself or your family. By the time anything happens, Jane, there could be another solution. It's not always given to us to see more than a step ahead. Right? Jane, I've said enough for the moment. It's too soon. Go in now, and sleep dreamlessly.'

He didn't kiss her, but she liked the look he gave her.

Jane went in, made a drink for Esmeralda, saw her to bed, told her laughingly she wasn't to read past midnight, and went to bed herself.

For once she didn't read. She lay back with the bedside lamp on, her hands behind her head, gazing at the funny match-lined old ceiling down which straw still dropped occasionally from the remnants of nests in the eaves, and dreamed.

'There could be another solution,' he had said. What was a girl to take from that? What dared she take?

A sort of singing happiness pervaded Jane. It seemed to throb in her veins. Maybe the years ahead needn't stretch out as a sturdy battle for the family, done in single harness. Broderic hadn't hesitated to assume responsibility for an old lady, so he wasn't the sort to quail before other responsibilities. If he thought my happiness depended upon

102

it, Jane thought, he'd keep on with the inconvenience of moving his stock from one side of his estate to the other via the main highway.

Another comforting thought came to her. Painting was something one didn't ever give up, so all through the years, whatever her state, she would be earning money of her own. Her mother would never have to think she alone had to support the twins ... even if I no longer lived down here, Jane thought, Broderic wouldn't turn them out, bulldoze this down ... with quite a sense of shock Jane realised where her dreams had taken her and was horrified. Good heavens ... one kiss and a couple of sentences that had appeared meaningful, and she was thinking in terms of marriage. Why? She knew the answer ... for the first time in her life she was in love. She reached over, snapped off the light and fulfilled Broderic's wish for her by falling straight into an exhausted sleep.

The days sped by, filled with tasks that were a delight in themselves, even if it often seemed there were never enough hours in the day. The little wayside stall became busier as the number of tourist buses increased. Broderic said to her, 'You won't have to pretend you need Kate's help. If you're going to keep on producing enough pictures you'll have to have more time for sketching and painting. I wish Kate could have come sooner, but she's like you, Jane Esmeralda, she has a hefty conscience. She won't leave till she can be replaced.'

'And you wouldn't like her any other way.'

'I guess so, only from the sound of her letters she's still fretting her heart out. Only a change of scene will do it, I think. Kate was the biggest tomboy and the maddest, merriest kid—such fun. Now her letters are flat. She tries hard, too hard, to sound philosophical.'

Jane said, 'I've a feeling she ought to have told this man why she was giving him up. I know it saved her pride the other way, but you never know—he might have rued the fact he'd played it up in Fiji, and even if they'd had a clanging row about it, it might have blown over.'

'I felt that too. I urged her to have it out with him, but it was no go. She was adamant, and there's a limit to how much a brother can interfere with the sister he adored, even if, like most brothers, he tormented the life out of her. Jane, girls confide in each other. If Kate tells you about it, would you advise her to come out with the truth?—but don't tell her I've told you about it.'

'I would do just that, but it must come spontaneously from her. She mustn't be made to feel I was waiting for her to confide.'

One day, right at the end of a selling session, Jane looked up to see someone she knew; someone who'd had a fairly prolonged holiday in Suva last year. He was broad and tall and had a tanned face that showed brownly against his fair hair.

'Why, Scott! What a surprise to see you here. Of all the tourists that have come into the shop, you're the first ever from Fiji.'

He laughed. 'It's even more of a surprise to find you so far from your own haunts. What made you leave Fiji?'

She told him. 'You'll remember Noel Eastwood, my father? Stepfather really. He did all the murals for that musical we put on, when you so ably stepped into Miles Hathaway's place when he broke his leg. He planned this, but died before we could put it into action, so Mother and I decided to do it ourselves, selling our own pictures.'

He gazed about him. 'I hadn't realised you painted like this, Jane. In fact I didn't know you painted at all. You were working as a waitress at the place where they staged that musical, weren't you?'

She nodded. 'I was just feeling my way towards becoming a full-time artist then, and this sort of scenery is more my right métier. Not the lush tropical stuff, charming though it is. It's been a big venture.' She made a gesture towards

Esmeralda, talking to some Canadians. 'See the delightful old lady over there? She's my step-grandmama—married my crusty old grandfather a few years ago. The pottery and novelties are hers. Mother and my sisters—I'm pretty sure you met the girls—are in Oamaru, and now I've proved this can pay, they're coming down here when the school year's finished.'

'Sounds ideal,' said Scott. 'I'm thrilled for you. I'd like to meet your step-gran when this crowd's gone.'

'Oh, aren't you with them?'

'No, I'm a company rep. I'm based in Invercargill, so this is my area. I'm on my way to do further north. As a matter of fact, though, I came to——'

At that moment Esmeralda came bustling up. Jane introduced them. 'This is Scott Mackenzie, Godmother, from Invercargill, but we knew each other in Fiji. Scott helped us out once in an emergency. Scott, we're putting up the shutters now. How about coming up for a cup of tea? Esmeralda made her delectable brand of girdle scones this afternoon earlier. With home-made butter and apple jelly they're out of this world. See . . .' She pointed out of the back window. 'We live up there, in that converted school . . . though we call it the Wedgwood House.'

He looked, said, 'I think that garden deserves the word delectable too. That brought me to a halt this afternoon. I thought I'd like to take some photographs of it, with your permission. They would be just wonderful for our catalogues. I travel for a firm of seed merchants. It beats your suburban gardens hollow.'

Esmeralda was charmed. She consented, then said, 'Are you related to the Mackenzies who used to live overlake from Queenstown, at Walter Peak? Because I'm sure I've heard that name before, Scott Mackenzie.'

He shook his head. 'No, my people have lived in Taranaki from pioneering days on. This is awfully good of you. It seems an age since lunch at Te Anau, though I'd like to take those photos first, while the sun's in this position.'

Esmeralda fell for him in a big way. He included her in some of the pictures too, and Jane. Esmeralda glowed at his praise of her garden. He said, 'That trellis of sweet peas —so early—is the most wonderful advert. How glad I am that they were our seeds. I'll mention that you added soot to the manure in the trench when you sowed them. That sundial too, with the nasturtiums wreathing round the pillar and all that aubretia and rosemary cascading over the loose-stone walls, is a perfect picture.'

He knew and loved his job; he felt his products created loveliness wherever they were used. They talked gardening techniques flat out. 'I'll come back tomorrow morning if I may—I've a call to pay down here in any case—back from Frankton, I mean. I'd like to take some shots of that sun-plant on the bank, but you need the morning sun full on it so that the flowers are completely open. I've never seen such a magnificent one. Would that be okay with you?'

Esmeralda said, 'Are you booked in anywhere, because if not, stay with us. There's plenty of room, as you can see. It would save you a journey of forty miles or so each way.'

'I'd like that very much,' said Scott, 'if it won't be too much bother. I know Jane's brand of hospitality of old and it would suit me well because——'

At which moment Broderic Adair walked in through the open door.

Esmeralda said happily, 'Oh, there you are, Rory. This is a friend of Jane's from Fiji; at least they met there. Scott Mackenzie.'

Jane saw Rory's face harden, the brows come down. His voice held no warmth. 'Oh, no need for an introduction, Esmeralda. This is Kate's ex-fiancé.'

Jane saw Scott take a grip on his feelings. He said quickly, in an attempted matter-of-fact tone, 'Oh, hullo, Rory. I was just saying it would suit me fine to stay the night here, as I wanted to see you. That's why I dropped in at the stall, to ask where was the lead-in to Starlight.' '

'Was it?' suggested Broderic, with an unbelieving rasp to

his voice. 'But of course you knew Jane was here?'

Jane was glad Scott didn't sound on the defensive. That would have been ridiculous. He merely sounded surprised. 'Why, no, I'd no idea she was even in New Zealand. Talk about a small world! You could have knocked me down with a feather when I spotted Jane.'

'What a nice surprise for you.' Broderic's voice sounded suave. What was bugging him?

Esmeralda came in. 'No wonder I thought the name was familiar, yet I didn't know your face.'

Still that dry rasping note in Broderic's voice. 'No, you didn't meet. You were to come down for a holiday with Kate, weren't you, Scott? Had you done so, you'd have met Esmeralda earlier and her garden would have made it into this year's catalogue. Instead you went off to Fiji. What a pity!'

A double meaning here. Had he not gone to Fiji he'd never have fallen for that girl there. Jane wondered who she'd been, if she could possibly have known her. Odd, he'd got so caught up in that musical, there hadn't seemed much time for dallying on the side.

Scott Mackenzie's tone suddenly went dry too. 'Oh, I don't know that it was a pity. It got my sister over a very rough patch. She'd become very depressed and we thought she was going to have a breakdown. But she got hold of herself there.' He turned to Jane. 'Your mother certainly helped her.' He said to Broderic, 'If you've met Willy, you'll know what a wonderful person she is. Jill was a different girl in the two weeks I left her in Suva on her own. Just the knowledge that Willy had been widowed as a young girl and had brought Jane up solo and eventually found happiness again gave Jill what she needed.

'Jill had always seemed so self-sufficient as a youngster that we hadn't realised that since her marriage she'd leaned heavily on Greg. Then, I'm afraid, I was over-protective. I coddled her too much, let her see my concern for her. I wasn't being bracing enough. Then the chance of this trip to one of the other islands with a bunch of guys and girls at the hotel came along. Willy advised me to take it, said I should give Jill the chance to realise she could look after herself in a strange country on her own. Willy said she'd keep an eye on her, but in the main would leave her to make her own amusements. She was a different person when I came back, despite my initial worries.'

'And did you worry about her all the time you were away?'

Jane wondered if Scott was as aware of the undercurrent sarcasm as she was. Could it be that this was when Scott had played up with the other girl?

Scott, unknowing, said with a grin, 'I thought I would. But after the first day, I came to the conclusion we must, at heart, be naturally self-centred, that we take the hub of our universe with us wherever we go. I had a rattling good time. I stopped being sore that I'd had to give up my holiday down here with Kate. I even planned I might take her to Fiji on honeymoon. Instead of which——' he turned out his hands in a helpless gesture. 'That's what I wanted to see you about, Rory.'

Rory was being purposely obtuse, Jane thought. Oh, he was what Esmeralda would call a thrawn de'il when the mood took him. He said, 'About what?'

Scott said, 'About Kate. What else? Can you spare me a bit of time?'

'I can. Right now. Jane, can I use your studio? It's more private than any other.'

It didn't take more than twenty minutes. They came out looking strained.

Broderic came through to the kitchen. 'I meant to tell you earlier, I'm eating over at Eyrewell's tonight. Sorry I forgot. But Scott can have my share.'

Jane said mildly, 'There'd have been plenty for everyone. We cooked a huge leg of mutton this morning to have cold with salad.' She turned to Scott. 'You'll enjoy Esmeralda's salads. She grows so many herbs I've never even heard of that every salad is an adventure in eating.'

Scott whipped out his notebook. 'Thank you, Jane. That last sentence will go under an illustration, complete with the recipe, I hope, for using those herbs, as grown from our seeds. So my call here hasn't been completely unprofitable, after all.'

Rory said, 'Oh, splendid. Then, seeing I wasn't as helpful, I'll bow out. I won't see you till tomorrow night, girls.'

Esmeralda bridged an awkward gap by saying, 'I find it odd that at eighty I can still appreciate being called girl. When I was young, I divided people into many categories ... the very young, the young, the not-so-young, the middle-aged, the elderly, the old, the antiquated. And you don't know till you've lived on borrowed time for a decade that you never really feel old inside. You still think of yourself as young and eager.'

Jane hugged her. 'Well, you do, anyway.'

Scott helped them with the dishes, and won Esmeralda's heart. Jane could see she was sorry that Kate had let him go. It was a spectacular sunset; from Esmeralda's house a long line of firs on the ridge of Eyrewell's property cut it off somewhat.

Scott said, 'Any chance of seeing that from higher up, Jane?' and Esmeralda said, 'Take him up Cruachan Beann, Jane, where Rory took you the other night.'

But that was what Jane, for some reason, didn't want to do.

She said quickly, 'I'll do better than that, Scott. We'll go out on the road, and back on to Starlight property and climb a little track there. It's easier going and you can see through Eyrewell's valley.'

She was wearing a cool sleeveless shift dress in beechy browns and greens, with a swinging Fijian girdle of slim bamboo segments and shells. They strolled along in silence, turned the corner past the ridge of firs, and here were the Eyrewells, mother, father, children, bidding farewell to Rhona Eyrewell's parents from Lumsden.

109

Jane greeted them and said without thinking, 'Oh, has Rory gone home?'

They looked surprised. Hugh said, 'We've not seen him today.'

Jane said hastily, 'Oh, trust me! I always get things mixed. I thought he was having dinner with you. He must have said Hamish, not Hugh.' She added, because these folk might know Kate's ex-fiancé's name if she introduced them, 'Well, mustn't hold you up—you've a longish drive ahead of you. So long.'

They were well out of earshot before Scott spoke. His voice would have outdone Broderic's at its most derisive. 'Well! It wouldn't be thin-skinned to take offence at that. What an extraordinary thing! I met Rory and liked him when he spent a week in Wanganui with his parents just after Kate and I got engaged. We'd gone over from Palmerston North. I liked him tremendously at that, looked forward to having him as a brother-in-law. I don't think the Adairs are my favourite people after all. They're inexplicable, moody. What the devil's the matter with them?

'I didn't dream when Kate ditched me they'd all take me in dislike, as if *I'd* jilted *her*. I don't know how much you know, Jane, but Kate came to the conclusion she didn't want to spend the rest of her life with me, so she wrote and told me so. I went to see her, of course, mad with hurt and disbelief, but she managed to convince me she was retrieving a mistake. I had to accept it.' His tone lost its dryness, sounded desolate. 'But I thought her brother would have been sorry. Sorry the engagement was broken, most of all sorry for me. I mean, it hurt me far more than it could have hurt Kate. I just can't get her out of my system, though I've tried. Every morning I wake up unable to believe that she's gone out of my life for good. I hoped Rory would be able to throw some light on it, that he might understand his sister better than I did.

'I feel Kate wasn't herself when the break occurred. Not *my* Kate. But Rory was so terse, like a closed book. He finished up by saying, "Look, you've got to accept the fact that Kate made this decision. Perhaps she found something in you ... or a lack of something ... that made her decide you weren't good husband material. And I'm damned if I think you ought to come to me for an explanation. Kate's the only one who can convince you." I'm baffled. I don't know where I went wrong. I wonder if I'd come down here with her for that holiday we'd planned, things might have gone differently.'

Jane wondered if Broderic's behaviour had been calculated to make Scott mad enough to tackle Kate on the subject. If so, she, Jane, ought to try to add to it. She said cautiously, because she must betray neither Rory's confidence, nor Kate's pride, 'I wonder if it was all a mistake—that holiday, I mean. It does seem to date from then, doesn't it? Can you think of any way in which you might have hurt her about that time?'

(Wouldn't it be splendid if Scott suddenly felt conscience-stricken and wondered if Kate could, by any ill chance, have heard about his holidaying behaviour? And decided to make a clean breast of it. Then Jane's thoughts slammed to a stop. There had been nothing whatever to cavil at in Scott's behaviour when in Suva. Had the tropical glamour of those more distant beaches on the island trip been too much for him?)

Scott said in a reflective way, 'There was only one thing that occurred to me. Did she feel I was the sort of chap who'd always put my own family first? But we were desperately worried about Jill. And Kate seemed to take it well, assured me she didn't mind a bit. She came down home and had her holiday, but only took a week in case I could wangle a bit of extra leave later, or even do relieving down here—I was stationed in the North Island then. She so wanted to show me all her favourite spots. But perhaps later she rather resented this. I could soon prove to her that my family is anything but possessive.'

He sounded eager, more hopeful.

Jane knew it wasn't that, but said thoughtfully, 'Scott, why not see her when you get back? This is only an idea and it could be way off beam, but if you accused her straight out of being jealous about you taking your sister on that trip, she might come out with whatever is really bugging her.'

By this time they were climbing the path that led to the ridge and they were silhouetted against the light. Scott turned and grabbed her hand, turned her round to him, gazed at her searchingly. 'Jane, you sound as if you really believe that it must be more than just a change of heart. I'll give it a go. Even if she storms at me, anything would be better than just existing without her. I wish someone had advised me to do that when I was still up north. Imagine being in the South Island when I decide to do something about it! Blast it, I'm fixed up for the next two weekends even, with the managers of various centres. Well, you say she's not coming down till nearly Christmas, so I can live through the next little while.'

Esmeralda said after Scott Mackenzie left the next morning, 'That's a nice young man. Pity he and Kate parted, but he seemed much happier when he left, almost elated.'

Jane nodded, not very happily. 'I think I was responsible, and it may not have been wise. I hope I've not raised his hopes only to have them dashed again. But he was so good with his sister, I can't imagine him not being a grand husband. Esmeralda, you know why Kate gave him up, I suppose?'

'Yes, but now I've met him I can't help wondering if that report was more malicious than true. This so-called friend of Kate's who spilled the beans; I don't know her, so can't tell. What did you do, Jane?'

Jane told her, and Esmeralda chuckled. 'It could well work. Don't you worry. Knowing Kate I reckon she'll get really mad if she's accused of being jealous of his holiday with his bereaved sister. And once you get mad, the truth comes out. Oh, she may have wanted to save her pride, but pride's a cold bedfellow.'

Jane decided not to take Broderic to task for his surliness. She was pretty sure it had been done with the best intentions. He came over that night, and Jane and Esmeralda had decided it would be better not to tell him they'd talked the situation out or what Jane had done.

When Esmeralda went out to water her asters, Broderic said, 'You seemed to know Scott pretty well. How come he didn't know you were here? Didn't you keep in touch?'

Jane blinked. 'Good heavens! He was just one among hundreds of tourists I'd met through the years. I knew him a bit more closely than some, certainly, because he very decently substituted for a chap who was in a musical we put on, and who broke his leg. Scott's a fine singer and knew every song, so he had a head start. I never thought about keeping in touch.'

'But if his sister stayed with your mother for a spell, didn't she write from N.Z. to thank her?'

'Oh, she didn't—stay, I mean. She just stayed on in the guesthouse, but Dad and Mum took her out in our boat, had her to meals once or twice. They had a few yarns together about adjusting to life when you were widowed, that's all. Broderic, may I say something? Could it be that Kate took gossip for gospel? I mean, there was absolutely no sign of any philandering on Scott's part any time I saw him. The practices for the musical took up a fair bit of his time, and if he'd been inclined that way there were quite a few unattached girls who'd have been only too keen. I'd suggest you tell Kate straight out that she ought to tell Scott her real reason for giving him up. Everyone deserves a fair trial. I can vouch for the time he was actually staying in Suva. I admit I can't on the island excursion. So?'

'I'll have to think about it, Jane. Kate's a cussed girl and has no confidence at all in her power to charm. But thanks.'

CHAPTER SIX

THEIR wish for Esmeralda to have some happy years with them as a family didn't come true. She died exactly one week later.

It had been a glorious day. No buses were scheduled to stop and Esmeralda and Jane had just pottered. Esmeralda had picked a bowl of roses, arranging them with all the artistry that was natural to her. She had wandered happily among her stone paths, picking here a spray of honeysuckle, there a sprig of balsam, squeezing them between her fingers and sniffing appreciatively. Later she had filled some herb jars and added fallen petals to her pot-pourri bowls.

The three of them dined off a delicious aspic mould that Jane had concocted the day before, with minced cold lamb and mint sauce and baby carrots and peas. They had had the first of their new potatoes, small and waxy, and a crisp salad with a trifle to follow.

Esmeralda said, 'Tom was very fond of trifle. He would have enjoyed this.' She bent over her plate and added quite matter-of-factly, 'I saw him today.'

Broderic and Jane were startled into exchanging alarmed glances over Esmeralda's white head. Was she getting a little senile?

Esmeralda didn't notice. She reached out for some more whipped cream, and sprinkled sugar lavishly. Still the same tone, not expecting them to doubt her. 'He was standing under the clematis arch. He hadn't changed a bit. He always loved that strain ... *montana rubens* ... Said no matter how large the other varieties were, the little one was the most generously prolific and the sweetest ... all those small pink stars. We had an arch just like that in Queenstown. Jane, what makes this trifle so delicious?'

Jane said, wisely deciding not to comment on the imagined appearance of Tom, 'I don't know. Let me see. Oh, just that after I sprinkle the sponge sparingly with sherry, I pour a little cooling liquid jelly over it and allow it to set before adding the fruit and custard.'

'That's it,' said Esmeralda happily, demolishing it.

Broderic and Jane washed up. Just as Jane let the dishwater go from the sink, Broderic put his arms about her and kissed her cheek, the first kiss since that evening up Cruachan Beann. With the promptness of a stage cue the door opened. Esmeralda! She beamed. 'Now, isn't that nice?' she said.

They both burst out laughing, though Jane went pink. Broderic said, grinning, 'Blushes beautifully, doesn't she, Esmeralda?'

Jane tossed the dishcloth at him, Broderic fielded it neatly and it fell into the sink, drenching Jane. 'Poetic justice,' he said.

Esmeralda made no apologies for intruding. 'I wanted you to thread my needle, Jane. I'll have to have my glasses changed again.'

They came through, and Esmeralda went on sewing little silk hand-made roses on her lavender bags. Jane was writing to her mother, Broderic began a letter to his. There was nothing worth watching on television.

'I like it that way sometimes,' said Esmeralda contentedly, 'It means one can settle to a book for two or three hours.'

Broderic cocked an eyebrow at her. 'Some gruey murder? Really, Esmeralda, your reading habits!'

She pulled a face at him and picked up a book from the table beside her for him to see the title. 'No, I've got out an old favourite—one of Beverley Nichols' garden books. I've never been to England to see any of his gardens, but I know every inch of them. They're as familiar to me as my own dear garden.'

Broderic said, 'Well, you certainly created beauty out of a wilderness here, Esmeralda. Just think how Jane's mother

115

and Louise and Lauris are going to love it. Jane, remind me to get the old basket swing chair out of the shed and mend it. I must swing it again from the big old apple tree before they come.'

They went on writing. Esmeralda occasionally read them a passage from the book, asked them if they thought they could burn some apple-wood in their fireplace the next cold night. 'Beverley Nichols says it's a wood of intoxicating fragrance.'

Broderic nodded. 'There's a big fallen branch under one of the trees in our orchard. I'll get Bernie to saw it up.'

Jane finished her letter, sealed the envelope, turned and looked at Esmeralda.

The next moment she was saying: 'Rory, Rory, I think she's—or is she still asleep?'

He sprang up immediately and went across to where Esmeralda was sitting with her head against the wing of the big chair, her feet on the footstool Jane had slid beneath them, the open book on her lap. She had a little smile on her face, but the smile was fixed.

Broderic felt her pulse, looked at Jane, said, 'Get me the hand-mirror off her duchesse, will you?'

She brought it back, gave it to him, leaned over with him ... the glass remained unclouded.

They both straightened up and looked at each other. Broderic moved round the chair, folded her against him so that her head was under his chin. His hand came to the back of her hair, stroked it gently. 'That's the way most of us would love to go, Jane, if we'd any choice.' His voice became husky. 'But how we'll miss her.'

Jane put her arms about him then, turned her face sideways, 'Oh, Broderic, she's been part of your life so long. I'm glad for her, but sad for us. For the girls too—they just loved her. What do we do now?'

'I'll ring her doctor. I'll get him to bring a nurse out to perform the last kindly offices for her.'

Jane realised Broderic and Esmeralda had talked over

116

just this eventuality long since. He knew her every wish. She wanted to be buried in the little kirkyard at Maunga-Whetu, within sight and sound of all she had loved so much, the mountains, the valleys, the wind in the larches and poplars, the birdsong ...

'It means, Jane, that she must stay here till the time of the service. If she'd been in Queenstown, she could have gone into the undertaker's chapel. How do you feel about that, Jane?'

She looked at him uncomprehendingly, then, 'Oh, do you mean I mind? Oh, no, Broderic. I've looked on death before, and Esmeralda must be here to the last among her flowers and her treasures.'

Broderic looked down, lifted one of the little white hands, bent his face to it. 'Oh, Jane, how fitting! Her hands are still fragrant from her lavender.' For a moment his voice broke, then steadied. Jane laid her own hands over his and Esmeralda's.

'And she was reading a garden book. I shan't be at all nervous through the night, or tomorrow night, either.'

Broderic said, 'Oh, I'll sleep down here. I'll get Lisel to come down to make it right. I won't leave you alone.'

Things moved slowly, with a minimum of fuss. Everyone, even the nurse, had known and loved Esmeralda. Broderic saw to the notices, rang people who must know before they saw them, and much later rang his parents in Wanganui and his sister in Palmerston North. His parents wouldn't be able to come, as Isabel had taken her pupils on a tramping trip now that their exams were over, and they had the care of her children. And Kate was down with 'flu.

Broderic said, 'It's rather late to ring your mother, Jane. It's very late and it might give her a disturbed night. It can't be in any paper she would see till tomorrow night.'

Lisel came down and retired to bed in the room that was to be Mother's. Broderic was to use one of the girls' beds. That left Jane in the one next to Esmeralda's. Before he went through the door in the conservatory he paused and looked at the paintings Jane had done of the features of the garden.

'I'm glad she saw those completed.' He took Jane's hand, said, 'And I'm glad she saw that little scene in the kitchen tonight. Goodnight, Jane.' His kiss was not a passionate one, but a long, tender one.

In her room, Jane met her mirrored eyes. He was glad Esmeralda had seen him kissing Jane. It meant—it *must* mean—that he was glad Esmeralda had had a glimpse into the future, their shared future. She couldn't see what else it could mean. Jane went to sleep comforted. What was it Mother always said? ... 'When one door closes, another opens.' So be it.

When she rang her mother, she got Louise. 'Mother's in bed with a tummy bug, but she's quite all right. She said on no account to let you know—but now you've rung you've got to know. But don't worry, we're managing fine. What did you want, Jane?'

Jane said: 'Is she well enough to come to the phone?' The twins would probably announce it dramatically in the manner of children, even though they'd be sorry not to have Esmeralda's company now. Mrs Eastwood came and was very sorry to hear the news, though agreeing it was a lovely way to go. She would have come through to be with Jane, but she couldn't travel, naturally. It was just something everyone at the home had had recently.

Jane found Broderic at her elbow. Jane put her hand over the mouthpiece. He said, 'Your mother may start worrying about an altered situation here. Tell her things can continue just the same. I ought to have told you that last night.'

'How can they? We were Esmeralda's tenants. We'll have to discuss that later when——'

Broderic said, 'But I'm telling you it will be all right, Jane. I can guarantee you can go on renting it.'

'But is that decision in your hands? Oh—you mean you're a trustee?'

'Yes, a trustee. Jane, you're on toll, I can't explain it all now. Just tell her that to save her worrying. I've other things in mind, but that will do to go on with.' His eyes met hers meaningly. Jane smiled back. He didn't want what he had to say to her to be all mixed up with a funeral and a deep sense of loss. People would be in and out all day.

She nodded, passed on the message.

They had the service in the Wedgwood House, not the church. Esmeralda's coffin was on the back verandah, with the glass doors pushed back so it was open to all the fragrance and sunshine and sounds of her loved garden ... bees humming, birds calling, the Adair Water singing on its way. Jane was mistily certain that Torquil Mayfield waited for his Esmeralda under the clematis arch. The minister, reading from the incomparable fourteenth chapter of St John, used the more intimate translation ... 'In my Father's House are many rooms ...' and Jane and Broderic exchanged a look in which was kinship of thought ... they would be rooms with windows opening on to fragrant gardens ... then the procession moved off, larger than Esmeralda would ever have dreamed, because half Queenstown was there, besides the local people, winding down the hill and along to the little white church where she had worshipped so often, to her rest under the soughing pines on the kirk rise where long ago Torquil's ashes had been scattered.

All the neighbours seemed bent on assuring Jane she had made Esmeralda's last weeks serenely happy. Inevitably they linked Rory's name with hers. 'You two young people meant so much to her,' they said. *We two*. Jane repeated to herself. It comforted her when every now and then the desolation of knowing she'd never again see Esmeralda stooping over her loved flowers, or coming in for her meals, would sweep over her.

Then they were gone and she and Lisel were washing up, Hamish and Broderic drying. The phone rang. Hamish called Jane. 'Oamaru calling.'

'It will be Mother, wanting to know how we fared.'

119

Hamish shook his head. 'No, it was a person-to-person, from Miss Louise Eastwood.'

Jane chuckled. 'How important that sounds! They'd probably toss up for the privilege of putting the call through. Though perhaps Mum's still weak from the tummy 'flu.'

The ones in the kitchen heard her voice change and they came to the doorway, concerned.

Jane had lost her colour. 'In hospital? When did they operate? *Yesterday?* You say she's all right? Louise, you must be frank. Was it serious? Oh, good girls, both of you. Keep that up ... I know you will, of course. But I'll come through right away. The twilight lasts till ten and it's still only four. But don't stay up—it will take me a little while to fix things here. I'll have a word with Lauris too. Right.'

Jane sounded very reassuring, as was right, speaking to two eleven-year-olds who had coped admirably with a scary situation, but when she hung up and turned round, Broderic got a chair under her quickly.

She smiled. 'I'm not going to flake out on you, it was just such a shock, and to be so far away. You'd hear enough to know Mother's undergone surgery, but it was just appendicitis. The trouble was she left it a bit late, putting it down to this prevalent bug, and they operated just in time to save her from peritonitis. Trust Mother! Last thing she said as they slid her into the ambulance was not to ring me till the funeral was over.'

Lisel said, 'There isn't one single thing for you to do before you leave. I shall do it all. But you must not hurry, *liebling*, through those gorges, or be so lost in anxiety that you lose your—your—— Hamish, what is the word I want?'

'Your concentration,' he filled in, 'but——'

Broderic struck in, 'But don't take the caravan, was that what you were going to say, Hamish? Take my car.'

Jane said apprehensively, 'But I'm used to the caravan. I'm a duffer with strange cars. Besides, I'll be a while nursing Mum even when she's out of hospital, and I'll need my gear to keep up my stocks. I can't hurry them. I mustn't be too

120

mercenary, but also I can't afford to waste time.'

He said unhappily, 'It's been such a big day for you already.' His brow cleared. 'I know. Hamish, the men can manage tonight. I'll drive the caravan through both gorges, as far as Clyde or Alex, and you can follow with the car and bring me back. Lisel, pack us a couple of flasks and some of those sandwiches and we'll have a snack together before we leave Jane. Won't take as long as a restaurant.'

Jane knew a great warmth at her heart.

Just before they reached Alexandra Broderic said, 'While I'm here I'd like to track down that girl who put Kate wise to Scott. I believe she's nursing in the North Island now, but her parents should still be here. Kate went to High School in Alex and knew her then. I've never met her. I don't think Kate had for years either. I can just imagine my sister getting so uptight about it, she wouldn't probe. What you said about Scott's behaviour in Suva has set me wondering. It's okay, Jane, I won't let on that you told me that.'

Jane said curiously, 'How come this girl knew about it? Was she on this cruise too?'

'Yes. Reckoned she saw enough to make her feel it her duty to warn Kate.'

Jane said, 'I'm never sure about the motives of people like that. It might bear investigation.'

'I think so. I'll have to write to her. It will take a lot of thinking out—what approach to make. Can't call her a probable liar.'

Jane said unhappily, 'Trouble is, if she did it just out of spite or jealousy, she'll probably not even answer you. It would be much better if Kate could bring herself to ask Scott right out. You could tell her that Scott came in to ask about her, saw me and I said I didn't think there could be a word of truth in it, because Scott was dancing attendance on his sister most of the time. Surely she'd go straight to Scott, then?'

'I'll have to think that out. Look, we'll pull into this

121

track leading into the pines, it's more private than in the town, to have our snack.' He signalled Hamish, close behind.

Both Hamish and Broderic kissed her goodbye, in brotherly fashion, but Broderic's farewell look lasted her many miles. Forbidding? Never. It had been only his anxiety, that Esmeralda might be let down again, that had occasioned it. She need never remember it again. It was impossible, even through her anxiety for her mother, not to dream of the happy future that lay ahead. Her mother and the twins would know real security if Jane married and lived at Starlight, just above them. Jane hoped that if there was another trustee for Esmeralda's estate, he would feel as Rory did and let them continue to rent. He seemed to have no doubts, anyway, when he'd reassured her mother so decidedly.

Jane found her mother much better than she'd expected, thankful that her elder daughter was home, and that the prospects for their future were so bright. Not that Jane had mentioned the brightest of all.

'You don't have to hustle to get better, Mother, I want you really fit before we travel. Oh, how you're going to love it! To live among such beauty is a bonus from fortune. I'll get out more, sketching, when you come. My store is dwindling, but only because they've sold so well. The money from those sales is safely in the bank earning interest. It's heavenly not to be living hand-to-mouth, and living's so much cheaper there, we live off the land so much. Broderic Adair came as far as Alexandra with me,' she went on. 'His man followed in his car. He says I'm to allow him to fill up the deep-freeze as often as of yore with mutton and beef. He'll also supply us with all our vegetables, and we'll just give him his dinner in return, though only till Kate arrives.'

She mentioned nothing of what Bernie had told her of the understanding that when Esmeralda died, Broderic had an option on the property, so that he could push an access road through. Jane knew with heart-sureness that for her sake Rory had given up that idea.

He rang her that night, and said, 'Broderic Torquil Adair calling one Jane Esmeralda Grey ... how are things with you? How is your mother?'

She told him. 'Good. Don't rush anything. We'll cope here. Get her strong and well, and if you feel it would be easier for her to come by air, take her to Dunedin and fly her in to Frankton. I'd meet her.'

'I think we'll wait till she's strong enough to travel with us. We'll do it in two stages—say, go as far as Lawrence the first day. Meanwhile I'll finish three pictures I've got sketched out and get things packed up here. Mother will be home in about another week.'

'Good show. Give her my regards and tell her I'm looking forward to meeting her. Well, now I know she—and you— are okay, I'm off on a brief trip up north. Won't say too much on the phone, local exchange and all that. So I'll just say look after yourselves and I'll ring when I get back, probably about Sunday.'

After he'd hung up she thought with vexation, she should have asked him something. She'd thought of it after she'd got home. If the friend who'd told Kate about Scott's lapse had been on that cruise and had been staying at the same guesthouse, then she might have met her, though half of them were putting up at another place. Never mind. If he was going to see Kate, it might all get straightened out anyway. Scott had said there was the possibility that this relieving position in Invercargill might become permanent. He wasn't going back up north as Kate had feared. Jane had warned Broderic not to tell Kate this.

He didn't ring Sunday, nor on Monday. Jane felt a little uneasy and told herself not to be such a wet-goose. He'd probably decided to write her instead, it was more private than on the phone. But even a postcard would have been something.

Tuesday and Wednesday passed too. Jane busied herself

looking after her mother now she was home. She was the most undemanding patient, lying happily reading, writing notes to friends in Fiji, or just sitting out on the back porch watching the opalescent sea beyond the rim of Oamaru houses.

Thursday brought a letter. She knew immediately that that black large, positive handwriting was Broderic's. Her heart gave the traditional leap of a girl in love. It wasn't going to be a newsy letter, though, it was too thin. Jane chided herself for that flicker of disappointment. How could she expect so much so soon?

She opened it hastily, glad that Willy was asleep, saw a letterheading bearing the enchanted words, 'Starlight Peaks', and wondered how long before she was using that letterheading for her correspondence; then her eyes dropped to the text. Next moment she was feeling sick with the nausea of shock and disbelief.

This couldn't be true. Broderic Adair wouldn't, couldn't, write anything as badly cruel as this.

'Dear Jane,' it began, which was hypocritical in view of what followed, 'I'm afraid circumstances have completely changed since you left and it is now impossible to offer you Wedgwood House to rent. As things have turned out, our former plans for this property must go through, namely through the area on which the school itself stands, to circumvent the Stumbling Block and to restore this estate to its earlier stock mobility efficiency. This, of course, was the reason I was not best pleased when Esmeralda so impulsively offered you a home with her, but I held my peace for her sake.

'However, Bernard says you know about the circumstances of the sale, so you won't really be taken too much by surprise. I'm sorry I allowed you to think it would be possible to establish yourselves here permanently, but things have been brought to my notice these last few days that force me to withdraw that offer. I realise this may have inconvenienced you, and I feel this was my fault for allowing my feelings to be swayed, so I am prepared to compensate you generously for that.' He mentioned a sum that Jane, had she been capable of clear thought at that moment, would have recognised as handsome, but fury was welling up in her to such an extent that it was a physical hurt.

'I'd like to suggest that as this district is so difficult to obtain rented houses in, you seek one in some other tourist-frequented area, possibly Fairlie, or Tekapo, in South Canterbury on the way to Mount Cook. Therefore I suggest I hold what few possessions you have here till you let me know where to send them, but I will forward, at my own cost, such things as you need immediately, to Oamaru. Just let me know.

'Yours faithfully,
'Broderic Adair.'

Jane had never before experienced such feelings of rage as possessed her. She'd heard of people seeing red, but was amazed when she actually did. When her vision steadied she was visited by a primitive desire to sieze that ugly lustre vase of the landlady's and hurl it clean through the nearest window. In the effort to repress this fury, she brought her top teeth down on her lower lip with such force that the next moment she had the salt taste of blood on her tongue. Then she walked sharply to the window and gripped the sill with her hands to stop her fingers trembling.

She took a deep breath, fumbled for the door-handle, walked out. Her mother was sound asleep and she must, she just must get some clean fresh air into her lungs. Blindly she turned down a street that led to the sea and when she came to an empty section, leaned on a tumbledown wall and stood there taking in great gulps of the cool sea-breeze.

The singing in her ears diminished, though not the pain in her heart. It was quite unbelievable. She'd thrust the letter deep into the pocket of her dress, and now she brought it up to read again. She shook, despising herself for such weakness. She'd had setbacks before ... but not from someone she loved. Loved deeply. Her mind turned inward on memory ... Rory standing with her on Cruachan Beann, kissing her. Again, a light kiss when she was standing at the sink, the tender words he'd spoken at the door of her room in the hours immediately following Esmeralda's death. He'd said, 'I'm glad she saw that little scene in the kitchen, Jane.' What else could he have meant but what she'd read into that?

To Jane's horror, a little sob escaped her. His concern lest her mother might feel their refuge would be gone now. She'd taken from that that it was within his power—as chief trustee—to continue to let this to them, that he would let his option lapse.

She wondered how Esmeralda had left the place in her will. She'd mentioned nephews of Torquil's in Australia—possibly it would go to them. Perhaps they were ready to let it go so cheaply that Broderic Adair hadn't been able to resist it. The desire for the return of that land must have swept away all feelings he had undoubtedly begun to feel for Jane Grey. How superficial those feelings must have been! The true Adair of Starlight had been that scowling, forbidding man she'd seen at first. Maybe he'd been not so much guarding Esmeralda's interests as acting watchdog for his own!

Jane forced herself to recover from the shock of it. It was a blow over the heart as far as she was concerned, yes, but she was not the only one to be considered. Willy wasn't in any state to hear news like this. At that thought Jane almost panicked. Then she steadied. She must play for time till Mother was stronger. She'd have to tell her eventually, but for the moment she'd say nothing. Much as she'd have liked to have written Broderic Adair the sort of letter that would have made him feel less than four feet high instead of six feet two, she'd just keep him waiting for an answer. She hoped it would worry him. He was one for quick decisions, so not knowing how she'd received the news would irk him. Good!

Her mind was like a beehive, turning over this possibility

and that. Where to go? It must be a tourist area, or it was back to waiting on tables again for her, on an existence wage. Unless she could persuade one of the shops here to sell her work on a commission basis, as an extra to what she could earn.

She must go back. Her mother would waken soon, the twins would come in from school, full of chatter about the delights that would be ahead of them, beyond the waters of Wakatipu, among the great southern mountains. Meantime ... when in doubt, say nowt!

Four days later, days in which Willy greatly improved, another letter reached Jane. But not from Broderic, though it was postmarked Queenstown. It was from a firm of solicitors.

Again Jane couldn't take it in, though this time the news was so good that she couldn't believe it. Her step-grand-mother had left her everything of which she died possessed, save a few keepsakes for Broderic Adair and his sister.

This time she collapsed on her bed. She'd taken the mail into her room every day since, in case Broderic had written again. The solicitors would like to see her when she returned to the area.

Jane took the rest of the mail to her mother, told her that she was walking into town for some painting requisites, and this time went to Friendly Bay, to sit on a seat watching the sheltered waters lapping gently at the edge.

She thought it out. *Wedgwood House was hers*. That agreement Broderic had seemed to possess re his right to repurchase must have lapsed, or else had been a word of mouth bond. So ... he'd managed to move his stock via the highway for two years since the new road went through, and by heaven, he was going to have to keep on doing it.

Yes, Jane was going to take possession of Wedgwood House all right, the Crafts Centre, the hillside garden. To the devil with Adair's steers, his sheep. It was all hers. Darling, darling Esmeralda! No having to tell Mother that the Broderic Adair she'd so liked the sound of had reneged on

127

his promise that they could still rent the property. There would be only rates to pay, and rates so far from city amenities were very low.

One thing and only one thing Jane flinched from ... the knowledge that she would have a hostile neighbour, a man she had once loved and now would distrust and dread. It would be as great, that hostility, on his side as on hers. It was no good trying to tell herself that the situation would improve once she was settled in, because Adair of Starlight was a man in whom she could repose no trust at all.

Jane rose, went into the town, bought a pad and envelopes and retired to the Post Office to write to her enemy. No good using a milder term, that's what he was, but Esmeralda's loving provision for her godchild had spiked his guns.

Her letter was terse. She told him she had, of course, been utterly astounded and disgusted at his letter, that never before had she come up against anyone so land-greedy that he could put the happiness and security of a whole family below his need for easy access to part of his own enormous estate.

Fortunately, she went on, the Fates seemed on her side and by this morning's mail she had received word from Esmeralda's solicitors that Esmeralda had left her everything of which she had did possessed, save a few keepsakes for himself and his sister; that the solicitor hadn't specified them, but which she, Jane, would hand over to them immediately he did.

She said that given other circumstances, she wouldn't have cared to live in such close proximity to so uncongenial a neighbour, but when one had family responsibilities, fine gestures like that were not to be indulged in. She just hoped they might see as little as possible of each other. She added that she hadn't told her mother and sisters of his letter, fortunately, because her mother had been in too weak a state just then, but now the true situation had been revealed and she was the owner of Wedgwood House, she was doubly

128

glad she had kept her own counsel. Her mother would be well enough to travel in about ten days, but they would not bother him at all. She signed it: 'Yours much more faithfully and honestly, J. E. Grey', and felt much better.

She knew she'd done the right thing when her mother wept for joy when Jane told her of their legacy.

She certainly hadn't expected another letter from Broderic, and she tightened her lips when she saw it. If he thought he could bring pressure to bear upon her, he was much mistaken.

When she'd read it through she was filled once more with anger and knew an even greater determination to stick to her guns. He stated quite calmly that he realised it must have been tempting when she heard she'd been left everything, but he was sure she would want to honour Esmeralda's pledge to him, that upon her demise, the Starlight Estate would be made one workable whole again.

He explained how sheltered that section was, that it was the very best pasture for his lambing ewes, but was rendered useless for that by lack of quick access from the farm. Until the new road had had to be brought close under the Stumbling Block, they had always used it, and he'd never have relinquished his option on the property to Esmeralda had he known that the road must go through there. He'd made one sacrifice because of the Eyrewells, but he'd not have made that had he not thought it meant being inconvenienced for only a few years. To be held up indefinitely or permanently was unthinkable in the circumstances.

Unthinkable, Jane repeated to herself. But he was going to *have* to think that unpalatable thought, because the land now belonged to Jane Grey and indubitably her need was greater than his, and her right unassailable. She read the next paragraph twice. It was just ridiculous. He was actually offering to buy it, and the amount, considering the price of land these days, was despicably low. What arrogance!

'You told me once that your aim was to be able to pay a

good deposit on a house. This amount would provide you with that deposit and you could hardly expect more for a hundred-year-old school. I'm sure you'll be able to find a small bungalow or cottage in some area suited to your needs. With a deposit like this you should be able to raise the rest of the finance easily enough. The time has come for this portion of the Adair estate to return to it. If you would consent to this, I'm sure it would be better for everyone. Hoping to have a favourable reply very shortly,

'Yours sincerely,

'Broderic T. Adair.'

Slowly Jane tore up the letter, her heart heavy, her purpose firm. He was not only a twister, a turncoat, he was a pinchpenny. Some men thought women gullible in matters of business. Well, Broderic Adair was going to have a shock when she turned up, unannounced, to take possession of her own property! She conceded him a natural resentment; he'd looked after Esmeralda for years, and now a stranger had scooped the pool, but her need was so great that she must look on this as meant to be. Oh, if only the Stumbling Block wasn't so impregnable. But it was as great a barrier as the Giant's Staircase had been all those years. Boundaries had made trouble ever since the world began, but she'd never thought to be involved herself in anything like this. Jane went ahead with her preparations, but no joy walked with her.

CHAPTER SEVEN

JANE was glad her family noticed nothing. Of course they were so busy packing that the hours were full. Willy was thinner, but she looked better, apart from that, than she had done for months; and Jane realised it was the freedom from worry that was putting the spring back in her step, the lilt in her voice.

So Jane switched off her apprehensions to a great extent as they neared Lake Wakatipu, because surely this had been the right thing to do, and since Wedgwood House, the Crafts Centre and its enchanting garden were now hers, no one could say them nay.

The beauty of the lake hushed even the babbling twins to silence, and Willy looked on it with serene eyes, saying now and then, 'I can't believe our incredible luck.'

The lake was with them for miles, ever-changing, ever lovely. 'Of course we're some miles past the foot of it,' she went on, 'but this is the road we use most, up and down to Queenstown. And the other way leads to all the wonders of Fiordland. Dad and I were fascinated with it. So we have a lot of exploring to do, other lakes to visit, and a fiord. And girls, in the season, when they bring the Kingston Flyer up from Lumsden, you can board a boat and go up-lake on it. I'll take you down to Lumsden one day and put you on the Flyer so you can have the thrill of a steam train.'

Louise said, 'It will be even better if that Rory takes us up in his launch—you said he kept one at Kingston. Because if there are no roads on the far side of the lake, it would be wonderful to have a private boat and be able to call in at the bays and homesteads there.'

Jane said crisply, 'You'll have to content yourselves with taking a day trip on the *Earnslaw* some time, the big steamer. Rory Adair has more to do than take us on the lake, he has a sheep-run to manage and is in a lot of community affairs.'

Lauris came to her sister's rescue. 'But it's been said that the busiest people have the most time to spare,' she observed quaintly.

'Well, not Rory Adair. He's not the kind you can kid round. He's busy and brusque and I'll thank you not to bother him. Wedgwood and Starlight are two different properties, and you're not to impose on our neighbours.'

Her mother glanced quickly at Jane. 'Good gracious ... surely you've not taken a scunner at the man, Jane! It's not like you. Think how kind he was when Esmeralda slipped away, saying we weren't to worry, that as a trustee he'd see we could still go on renting it. I expect he was very happy when Esmeralda left it to you, Jane, so we had it free and it raised no problems.'

Jane felt weak ... *no problems*! She said, 'Well, I sort of had the feeling he'd done his duty nobly by Esmeralda, and though he was kind enough at the time of her passing, he hoped now to have no responsibility towards this gaggle of females arriving with no man to shoulder the chores that normally fall to the males of the household. What are you two giggling about?'

'At you, loved sister,' said Louise. 'You talk just like a book. That poor man! You just don't know how to handle men, Jane, you're so independent. And with your looks, you could have them eating out of your hand.'

Jane heard her mother begin to giggle too and said grimly, 'Well, perhaps I should take lessons from you two worldly-wise damsels. Look, there's the little village of Kingston nestling beneath the mountains at the foot of the lake. Not long now. But mind, just because Wedgwood House has a romantic sound, don't expect a mansion. It is, after all, just a converted school.'

They drove on down the road that ran now between widening flats and Jane pointed out where once, long ago, the lake outlet had been. A signpost said 'To Fairlight', and

Louise said, 'Oh, when will one say "To Starlight"?'

Beyond Garston the road curved round, big escarpments of rocks began to herald a change in contour, and in turn became the purple and slate-blue upthrusts of Starlight Peaks, which could always be seen long before the bend in the road brought a sight of the Starlight homestead gates with a thistle-head adorning each pillar, and almost immediately after the curved-back greensward, in front of the Crafts Centre, and the vision of glory and fragrance that was Esmeralda's garden.

Louise's cry of rapture at the sight softened suddenly to a bleak cry of desolation. 'Oh, Mummy, Mummy, if only *she* was here—Granny.'

Jane bit her lip to still its quiver and blinked hastily. Oh, yes, if only Esmeralda was here! Even if Wedgwood House wouldn't have been their own, under the aegis of her care and love there would have been no cruel move to prevent them taking up residence.

She stopped in front of the house, on the terrace above the rocky beds that spilled their purple, pink, and white cascades of tiny blooms downwards, took out the key, assumed a gaiety she was far from feeling and said, 'Ha! The Eastwood clan is upon its native heath ... let no man say it nay!' and turned the key.

The children were enchanted ... why had Jane warned them not to expect too much? What a heavenly corridor—well, conservatory—what fun this would be on wet days. And all those doors. Oh, super, there was even an inset blackboard in their room still. And what cupboards ... how tidy they would be here! They whisked in and out till Jane and her mother felt almost dizzy with their exclaiming and laughing.

Finally they got them quieted and despatched them to bring the carton of groceries from the caravan and began to set out their first meal in their very own home, a cold chicken they'd brought from Lawrence, a tossed salad sprinkled with Esmeralda's herbs and tiny succulent radishes from the garden, and crisp twisty rolls. How good freshly brewed tea was, after flasks of coffee on the journey. Jane suddenly felt more lighthearted, and some of the bone-weariness that had possessed her for ten days fell away.

She was delighted with the colour in her mother's cheeks, the youthful eagerness of her as she went from room to room, pausing constantly to look out of the windows with the beauty-loving eyes of the artist. She turned to Jane. 'Truly, our lines have fallen in pleasant places.'

They washed up, all helping, before going outside in the summer twilight to explore their domain, 'But we'll put the sheets on our beds first,' said Jane, 'because I know we'll not get you in for hours, once you get outside. However, while we do that, you can feed the chooks. I notice they're not out on free range, so I expect Lisel told Josef and Gretchen to keep them in their runs in case they got into the garden. They were probably fed after school, but you can give them a little now, to get to know them.

'The fowlhouses are past those steps between the tool-shed and the old barn. Go into the barn and dip up some wheat out of the old copper with a pan you'll find there. Be sure to put the lid back on tightly so no mice get in. Don't dare explore the loft, though; it's a very rickety ladder and is to be mended. Mr Adair warned me. He hadn't got round to doing it. He's not a man I'd care to disobey, so mind!'

They rushed off happily. Willy watched them smiling. 'So much for them to do! How glad I am for them. A country childhood is such a blessing.'

They'd just started on the first bed when the twins were back, flying in the door helter-skelter, alarm written all over whitened faces. They gasped out, in turn, as always, 'There's a man up there . . . he's hurt, he's not speaking. The ladder's all smashed up. His face is all blood and his arm is funny!'

It was no use telling Willy not to run, she was right be-hind them as they reached the barn. Jane was leading. The westering sun was striking strongly through the window, sending a shaft of revealing light across the crumpled form

134

on the stone floor. It was Broderic Adair.

Jane dropped on her knees, gazed horrified at his face. He must have been here some time ... that blood was congealed. Her mother, with the professional touch she'd acquired with her nurse-aiding, felt for his pulse. Her voice was relieved. 'It's a bit feeble, but not too bad. It's very likely just concussion, not a fractured skull. Oh, but he's cold, yet it's been a hot day. I think he's been here some time and is in shock.'

Jane said, 'Girls, beyond the hen-run is a little track leading through a spinney. When you get through it you'll see a brown house, that's Hamish Mackenzie's. Tell him Rory has fallen from the loft and seems to be unconscious. He must ring a doctor immediately. Both of you go. Mother will stay here and I'll get hot-water bottles and blankets. We dare not move him. Will that be right, Mum?'

Willy nodded, 'And if you can bring some warm water and a flannel, we may be able to sponge some of this blood away gently to see what damage has been done. But bring the blankets first, and leave the kettle to boil.'

Jane flew. Here was a complication! She was aware of feelings she couldn't analyse. She grabbed towels and face-cloths and ran uphill again. Broderic hadn't stirred, and her mother was gently chafing his cold hands.

They put the blankets over him, tucking them in, but not daring to push them under in case of internal damage. They each took a flannel and gently wiped away the dried blood from the lower part of his face, revealing little damage there beyond grazing. They worked upwards. He didn't as much as twitch an eyelid. There was a nasty gash on one cheek that seemed to be the source of most of the gore, but it now oozed only a little under their ministrations. The rest had come from a smaller cut on one temple, but that had an ugly area of bruising around it. 'That's probably what accounts for him being out to it,' said Willy. 'I'm glad to see he's not bleeding from the ears, but I think that arm could be broken. I won't touch it.'

In came Lisel, with first-aid kit, pillows and more blankets, followed by the girls. She said, 'Hamish is ringing for a doctor, but it takes time to get here, you understand. But for what did he go up that crazy ladder? Oh ... the bill-hook. See! Just this morning he said he'd hunt out the old one from the barn here. He said the steel in the old ones was better than in the new, that he'd sharpen this one.' Her eyes fastened on the cut on Rory's cheek. 'But it was sharp enough, *ja*. But Hamish is well trained. As soon as he has reached a doctor on the wire, he will be here and decide what must be done. So this is your mama, Jane? She looks, too, as if she knows something about nursing.'

Hamish arrived, paler than usual under his tan. 'The doctor at Lumsden is bringing a baby into the world, and it's a complicated job. There's been a flying accident in the mountains back of Queenstown, so one doctor from there is away up the Macetown Track at the moment, and the other's been called to Glenorchy. So both of those are hopeless.'

Hamish had a sure touch, his course of first aid must have been very thorough, even though he knew his limitations. He said, 'I think the only real damage to the head is the temple. I don't think he could have fallen on the back of it and received a bruise like that on the front, so it's possibly not as serious as it might be.' He gave his attention to the arm, lying at a very awkward angle. 'H'mm. I don't think this is broken, but it could be dislocated.' He exerted a little pressure on the shoulder and there was the faintest suggestion of a wincing away. Hamish looked sharply at his boss's face. 'He felt that ... very slightly. Good. He may be coming out of it. It may be hours before a doctor gets here—I think we'll be best to move him into the house, but we'll have to be mighty careful.

'Girls, Josef has gone for Bernie and Mick—praise the saints they stayed on tonight—but Gretchen is watching the baby. She knows where our camp stretcher is. Tell her we want the very low one and get her to give it to you. Jane, there's a piece of hardboard standing against the laundry wall. Bring it here. If we could slide that under him, then lift it on to the stretcher, we could get him down to the house with little disturbance.'

Jane brought the hot-water bottles back too, and they placed them one each side of Broderic. His pulse seemed a little stronger. Bernie, Mick, and the girls appeared, then Josef followed. They were extremely careful, sliding the hardboard under inch by inch, with Willy holding the arm as rigid as possible. Hamish had assured himself that no ribs were broken.

They took the corners, Jane making the fourth, and got him on the stretcher, then made their slow way down the steps and the slope below. They knew a terrific relief when they got him off the stretcher on to the bed.

'We'll leave him on the hardboard,' decided Hamish. 'The bed might sag a little, and if there should be any internal injury, that mightn't help. Well, at least he's off that stone floor.'

They cleaned Broderic's face more expertly, and put a dressing on the wound. It would need stitching if it weren't to leave a thick scar. Not even an eyelid flickered, so the other sign must have been only a momentary lifting of his unconsciousness.

No one had seen him since half-past two; Bernie thought he might have gone over to Eyrewell's because of something he'd said. They'd hollered out for him at dinner-time, but thought he'd be in soon. 'We might later have scoured the crags and gullies for him. We wouldn't have looked down here,' Hamish said, 'what a blessing Jane came back today.'

Jane drew in a deep breath of relief. That didn't sound as if *he* thought she had no right to be here. Then Lisel said, 'Rory said it was possible that after all you might not come back, that you were thinking you might take a place some-where else, in one of the tourist centres.'

Jane said smoothly, 'I did wonder about that, but then when I found Esmeralda had left me the whole lot, house, furniture, the shop, nothing could have been more ideal.'

A strange stillness seemed to strike the three men and Lisel. They looked startled, even embarrassed; then, the urgency of the present situation recalling them to matters in hand, they began talking of Rory and what had befallen him. Jane realised that though they might not know of the acrimonious exchange of letters, they must know that Rory had planned on being able to have access to the far paddocks again.

They'd switched on a heater and Broderic seemed less cold now. Jane found herself almost rigid watching for signs of returning consciousness. She felt as if the enmity between them had been suspended, that the only thing that mattered was for that stillness and remoteness to become movement and awareness. It was always uncanny to see someone unconscious. It made you wonder in what strange regions that withdrawn spirit wandered.

Lisel said, 'Jane this isn't good for your mother. It is so soon since that she is a patient in a hospital herself. Today she's had a long drive. It is not fit she should be tending the sick. She must go to lie down.'

Willy said, 'No, Lisel. It's been a lovely day till now. I did no driving, and the waysides were so beautiful I thought I was in heaven. Then the lake and sky, matching in blueness, and the mountains and trees and, at the end, Esmeralda's garden. The only thing that hurt me was that I had known her so short a time. How different things might have been had I known her when she first married my father-in-law. Yet to have known her at all was a privilege. I can certainly watch here with Jane. My experience these last few weeks will be of some use. You have your children up at the house, Lisel. I think I'd be glad if Hamish would stay till the doctor comes, because if Rory comes to, it will be good for him to see a familiar face—well, he knows Jane, but he's known Hamish longer.'

Jane thought grimly that hers would be the last face he'd want to see, and she had a moment of alarm wondering

138

how it would affect him. He could be angry, and that wouldn't help a man who'd just regained consciousness.

Hamish said, 'I'll sit beside him while you go and get your beds made up. Lisel, you could go home now. Oh, I've an idea! This has been a bad start for Louise and Lauris, and there'll be a lot of coming and going tonight. How about them sleeping up at our place? And Bernie, and Mick, would you go up to the homestead, check that everything's okay up there, and lock up? You can come back here again —you may be needed.'

The men started to go out of the room, paused, and Mick said, 'We'll see to the dogs up there and feed the cats. We'll be back for sure.' He looked at the inert figure on the bed. 'Gosh ... if anything should happen to *him*. Chap with a heart of gold.' They went out.

Hamish said gruffly, 'He's taken worse cracks on the rugger field, he's a tough hombre. But I know how they feel about him. If his shoulder's dislocated he could have passed out with the pain of trying to move—it's a hellish pain, I know. He'll be okay soon, I'm sure.'

They were well aware that this state of Broderic's was more than flaking out from pain, but Hamish was trying to comfort them. The men had been gone just a quarter of an hour when the doctor's wife from Lumsden rang. Good news ... her husband was now on his way.

It still seemed ages before he got there. Willy had changed into a white nylon overall. She said to Hamish, 'I don't think it'll be good for him to come to suddenly and find a stranger here, but if I'm in this, he'll take me for a nurse and won't have to pucker his brow trying to figure me out.'

Jane said, 'By the same token, I suppose it would be better if I wasn't in the picture. He wasn't exactly expecting me.'

Her eyes and Hamish's met fairly and squarely. His tone was even deliberate. 'No, that's true.'

Before he could add to that, Jane said, before her mother could come back from changing into soft slippers, 'Rory had the quaint idea he could buy this place from me. As if

I'd part with the ideal solution to our living problems. You'd better know, Hamish, that I said nothing to Mother about his offer. She was just out of hospital and had had one blow after another this year, and I wasn't prepared to deal her another. I don't want it as much as mentioned to her. But equally, I don't want to run the risk of upsetting your boss by having him see me the moment he regains consciousness.'

Hamish had opened his mouth as if to interrupt her half-way through, but had closed it again. Then he said, as if he were at a loss but must excuse his employer, 'You see, he'd set his heart on Starlight being an undivided property again. Don't hold it against him, he's a good fellow.'

They all thought that. Jane thought: *Good fellow!* She had the feeling the loyal but kindly Hamish might have had a shock had he seen the letter the good fellow had written her. But she said crisply, 'I just thought I'd mention it so you'll let nothing slip to Mother, poor darling. It's not just the roof over our heads, but with that shop at the gate, it's our livelihood.'

Hamish nodded. 'I guess things will sort themselves out and nothing controversial can be brought up till he's on his feet again. Hullo ... I think I hear the doctor. You've met him before, of course.'

Jane went out with Hamish to greet him and acquaint him with details. A great weight rolled off them as they watched his expert fingers at work.

'Shoulder's dislocated all right. I'd like to get it back before he comes round.' It was little short of magic. It would be painful enough for some time to come, with the wrenched muscles, but not agonising as when it was out. Jane saw Broderic's face twitch as it went back in. The doctor did too. He said, 'With a bit of luck I'll get his face stitched before he's round, save him the after-effects of a local. He'll have enough to put up with as it is.' He looked at Willy with approval. 'You made a good job of the cleaning-up.' He stitched it with incredible speed, then he examined the head

140

again, more slowly. They were relieved when he said there appeared to be no fracture, unless it was a hairline one. 'We certainly won't move him into hospital tonight. Later he can have X-rays taken, but he's best here. He's lucky having a nurse-aide on the spot. It's just concussion. He ought to be out of it soon.'

Jane said, 'Doctor, would you like some coffee and a snack? You've quite a drive back and like all doctors, I guess you're never sure of a good night's rest ahead.'

He agreed. 'I sure would like it. It's been a helluva day. I missed out completely on dinner.'

Jane said, 'How about a bowl of soup—only tinned, I'm afraid—and some cold chicken with, say, a couple of poached eggs? You can't carry on without stoking up.'

He grinned at her. 'A true successor to Esmeralda! She was always spot on. I sometimes called in here on my way back from Queenstown and she always rustled something up.'

Jane left the room with him. Reaction was setting in and she was glad to have something to do. The doctor said, 'Just at the kitchen table, thanks,' and sat down with a prodigious sigh, then went on talking about his day as she whipped up the light meal. He made her join him with the coffee. 'You can take the others some later. You must have had quite a day yourself if you've driven from Lawrence.'

She nodded, and joined him. 'I'll leave the percolator on —the men are playing cards in the lounge. They won't leave till they've heard what you had to say. In fact, till he regains consciousness, I imagine.'

The doctor, replete, had just sat back when Hamish came in quickly. 'He's coming to. His eyelids flickered and he moaned. First thing his eyes focused on was your mother. He said: "Am I in Frankton Hospital, then?" Before she could speak his eyes roamed round and he said, "That's funny, I'm at Esmeralda's," so your mother said, "I'm Willy Eastwood, Jane's mother. We arrived, found you, and we're looking after you. The doctor's here. Just lie still."'

Jane waited in the kitchen and the men came through. Jane told them Rory was round. They decided that the house would be better quiet, and went on up to their quarters. Jane sat on at the table, her head in her hands. She thought she heard a car stop outside. But who?—the door flew open and a tall chestnut-haired girl walked in. She said blankly, 'What's going on? Starlight's all locked up and there's a blaze of lights on here and a caravan parked outside. Who are you?'

Jane said, 'I'm Jane Grey. We live here. I seem to have seen you somewhere before, but——'

'I'm Kate Adair. Jane? That was the name of the girl Esmeralda had here. But I thought she—you—had gone. Rory said you lived in Oamaru and had gone back there. Is he letting you stay on?'

Letting? They all seemed to have this touch of arrogance. These high-and-mighty Adairs! Jane said quickly, without any hint of resentment, however, because this girl was going to receive bad news, 'Well, you see, my step-grandmother left me this place. So we arrived today, my widowed mother and my little sisters. But I'm afraid I must tell you we found your brother in the barn. He'd crashed off the ladder and dislocated his shoulder; he'd knocked himself out too. The doctor's with him right now. Broderic's in Esmeralda's room. He's just come round.'

Kate stared. 'Oh, what a good job you'd arrived right then. How is he? I'll go to——'

Jane said quickly, 'I'd better put you in the picture a bit more. He's not a pretty sight at the moment. His face had to be stitched, but it's not a long cut. He's got a small wound on his temple but a hefty bruise round it. No other apparent damage to his head. He's to rest tonight. My mother's a nurse-aide and will be a great help.'

The girl's look was all concern. 'I'd better not go in till the doctor gives me the all-clear. To burst in on him if he's just come to wouldn't be the thing at all. He's not expecting me for a couple of days yet. I was staying with friends in

142

Oamaru on the way, but they were called up to Christchurch, so I thought I'd surprise Rory and find out what sort of fist he'd made of the bachelor housekeeping.' She grinned. 'I guessed he'd have a great set-to the day before I arrived and have it all shipshape and Bristol fashion and I'd feel superfluous! I meant to arrive at a respectable time, but I called on friends at Alex, and you know how it is, it doesn't take long to stay two hours! Is that the doctor coming out now?'

It was. Hamish was with him. Doctor Femmingdale looked surprised. 'Kate? Last time I heard you were a physiotherapist in Palmerston North.'

She pulled a face. 'I made a surprise entrance ten minutes ago, and Jane has been putting me in the picture. Surprise is right, with poor Rory knocked out. How is he, Bruce?'

'Conscious but woozy. Don't barge in too suddenly. But this is good, you're next best thing to a trained nurse. I'll call back tomorrow morning. I've given Mrs Eastwood the gen, but I'll repeat it to you. I want someone sitting with him all night. Call me if you're at all worried, but I'm pretty sure he'll be okay now. Thanks for the meal, Miss Grey,' and he was gone.

Jane said to Kate, 'I won't come in with you. He doesn't know I'm here yet, and he might wonder.' Wonder? The understatement of the year. He'd be furious. She added, 'But when you've seen him, come out and I'll knock you up a snack. You must be tired.'

Kate began to thank her, then something struck her. 'But what must *you* feel like? You were travelling all day too. Then you had the shock of finding him and all the hooha since. I'll get myself something, thanks.'

Kate went along to the sick-room, came back, said, 'He's a bit wandery, but his pulse is quite strong. He recognised me, said, "Kate! Have I been out to it a couple of days, then?" I assured him he hadn't, that I'd arrived ahead of time and what a welcome to give me. I added it was a blessing Jane had come when she did. He looked a bit puzzled and said, looking at your mother, "That's right. She said she was Jane's mother," then he must have got confused because he said, "Round one to Jane ... spiked my guns, can't throw her out now, can I?" Your mother looked puzzled too. He shut his eyes and as he drifted off he muttered, "Tried to stop you two meeting ... poor show." What could he mean by that?'

Jane said honestly, 'I've no idea,' but she meant the latter remark, not the former. *That* she knew only too well. But the fact that he now knew she was here solved something. She said, 'My mother had her appendix out recently, and with you here, I don't think she ought to take a stint of watching. I don't want her having a setback. I feel wide awake—how about you turning in now, and I'll wake you at four and have some sleep myself?'

Kate said, 'I'll take that offer. If I watch all night I might fall asleep, but Jane, any change in him and you'll call me, won't you?'

'I promise.' When Jane went in to tell her mother she found Broderic Adair had fallen into a natural sleep. Those hours at his bed were strange ones. Never in her wildest dreams, since getting that first cruel letter, had she imagined a scene like this; watching him sleep, looking, for some reason, perhaps because of the defencelessness of sleep, younger and more vulnerable. A longing swept Jane to turn back the clock. She wanted Esmeralda back, wanted that night to return when she and Broderic had looked into the sunset from the crags of Cruachan Beann and had experienced a moment of enchantment.

It must have been just a mood-of-the-moment attraction for him. It meant less than nothing when it became apparent that she, the new owner of Wedgwood, stood between him and 'restoring the estate to its former stock-mobility efficiency'. What pomposity! What gobbledegook. Why couldn't he just have said: 'easy to run'? She'd still have got the message. What a fool she'd been to read so much into three kisses and an emotion-charged remark the night Esmeralda died!

She tried to read a book beside the bedside light round which her mother had tied brown paper on the patient's side to shield his eyes from the glare. Jane found it made her drowsy, so she slipped out for her knitting. She knitted for some time.

Suddenly he spoke, his voice faint. 'May I have some water, please?'

She picked up the glass, knelt by the bed, raised his head a little. He sipped thirstily. 'Don't gulp,' she said, 'you might choke on it and to cough would hurt your head.'

He turned, tried to focus on her. 'That's not Kate, it's Jane.'

She said lightly, 'I'm here till four, then Kate takes over. She's sleeping in one of the girls' beds just now. Don't talk, settle down again. Sleep's what you need most.'

Obediently he lapsed. It was more than an hour before he woke again. This time his eyes looked clearer, though his voice was still weak. He said, 'Did Kate mind?'

'Mind? She was horrified, as we all were, to think you'd hurt yourself and had lain so long unattended.'

'Not that.' He instinctively tried to shake his head and winced. 'I meant at finding *you* here. Was she upset?'

'Of course not. I expect, like you, she'd rather Esmeralda had left the place to you, but she thought it positively providential we'd arrived when we did. Hamish said they'd never have looked for you down here.'

'But when she recognised you?'

Jane felt vaguely alarmed. 'Oh, look, I think I'll get Kate. She's got more know-how than I have; I've a feeling you're delirious.' She put a cool hand on his brow. 'Odd, you don't seem feverish. Must have been the crack on the head. How could she recognise me?'

He said slowly as if it were hard to work out, 'Then she couldn't have seen it. Good. No, don't get her. I'm sleepy.'

A moment or two later he spoke again, eyes closed. 'Don't mention Fiji to her.'

Jane wished he'd drop off. She said crisply, 'I already have. She asked me where we'd lived before. Broderic, I'm sure she's not as sensitive as that. And you mustn't talk. I expect you've been so anxious about her, it's uppermost in your mind.'

His voice became stronger. 'I *won't* go to sleep. I want you to tell me what injuries I've got, how long I'll be out of circulation.'

Well, she didn't mind that. His hand came to his cheek. 'I've got plaster here ... and here.' His fingers went to his temple.

She said hastily, 'Don't attempt to move your other hand. You probably can't, because the doctor strapped you up pretty firmly, but you'd dislocated your shoulder. We think you fell on your temple and got concussion. Your cheek is gashed, but not badly. It's all stitched up. In some ways you were lucky.'

'I'll say, I might have fallen on that billhook. Damn silly thing to do. Should have fetched another ladder.'

Jane said, 'I'd better warn you of something. My mother knows nothing of your letters. She wasn't well enough to have any worry and as far as she's concerned, Esmeralda left me this place and we're staying. You mustn't argue about it. No matter what you offered, you couldn't buy us out. I'll sponge your face again and give you another drink. We didn't get all the dried blood off for fear of making bad worse, but now you can tell me if I hurt.'

She did it gently. He was getting drowsy again. Just before he slipped off he said, without opening his eyes, 'I know what Walter Scott meant now ... "O Woman! In our hours of ease, uncertain, coy and hard to please ... When pain and anguish wring the brow, a ministering angel thou." '

Jane looked up to see Kate in the doorway. Kate who was boggling, 'Hark at my brother ... quoting poetry!'

Jane said quickly, 'He's a bit lightheaded, I think. I tried

146

to stop him talking, Kate. He even burbled something about being surprised you'd not recognised me. How could you? He's not hot enough to be delirious.'

'It'll be the crack on the head. He's wandering.'

'I'm not,' said Broderic childishly. 'Didn't you see Jane's photo, Kate?'

'Photo? Where? Have you got one of her at the house? But I couldn't get in, it was all locked up.'

Jane laughed. 'He hasn't a photo of me. No reason why he should—I do wish he'd stop this and go to sleep. I think I'm disturbing him. I'll away to my bed. Sing out if you need me.'

It was well that Jane was exhausted and fell asleep right away and didn't wake till eight when she found her mother smiling beside her, a cup of tea in her hand.

'Not to feel guilty, Jane, I feel surprisingly well again. I can pull my weight from now on. Kate reports Rory slept from the time you left her. She's spooning bread-and-milk into him now and he's so anti what he calls pap, she's sure he's on the mend.'

Jane showered, dressed, went in. Broderic, washed, but still with a towel tucked round his neck, looked slightly sheepish. 'All right, Sis, I admit I feel better for swallowing that revolting stuff, but by tonight I hope I can manage a steak.'

'Steak!' Kate was scandalised. 'You'll get by on a poached egg . . . if you're lucky. You might, of course, be in Frankton Hospital by then, and I just wish them joy of you, that's all. You're going to be a shocking patient!'

He scowled. 'I thought women *liked* nursing men.'

Kate chuckled. 'You've a lot of peculiar ideas about women. About us being uncertain, coy, and hard to please! So even if pain and anguish *are* wringing your brow, we're not always ministering angels like you said last night . . . unless our patients behave themselves.'

'Like I said last night? What d'ye mean? I thought I was out to it most of the time?'

Kate said, 'When I arrived at three-thirty you were quoting that to Jane. She's softer than I am—I'd a fair idea you were off your head, so I just shut you up.'

Jane felt dismayed. What if he remembered nothing of what they'd said last night? Kate looked out of the window, said, 'Oh, here's Hamish, I'll be back in a moment.'

Jane came near the bed, said in a low voice, 'I hope you remember what I told you last night. Mother has no knowledge of the fact that you wanted to buy this land from us. She's not to know, ever. This is ours and here's where we're staying. I don't want to upset you so soon after your accident, but I must protect my mother.'

Kate came back in and said, 'Jane, I'd like to get that blood-stained singlet off Rory and a pyjama jacket on one arm at least. Hamish came down here at six and I asked him to bring down some of Rory's own things later. I think those pyjama trousers must be Hamish's.'

Rory looked horrified. 'Who got me into these?' he demanded, his uneasy gaze on Jane.

She said calmly, 'Hamish and my mother. Don't flap.'

She and Kate looked at each other and burst into laughter. 'My prudish little brother!' said Kate.

Jane knew a lift of the heart. She and Kate were going to be friends.

CHAPTER EIGHT

DOCTOR FEMMINGDALE was pleased with his patient's progress. 'But that doesn't mean you're in the clear yet, Brod. I know what you big husky fellows are like. Not being used to illness, you think you can get up and into normal gear within an hour of being allowed up. It's best to stay here the next few days where you've got Mrs Eastwood and Jane to relieve your sister, otherwise she'd be tied to you and I know what it'd be. She'd just be out of the room ten minutes and you'd be up and prowling round. A light diet for the next few days, then when I think you can stand it, Kate can drive you up to Queenstown for X-rays. You've got to take things very quietly.'

'Quietly? . . . have a heart! We've got the shearers coming in at the end of the week.'

'So what? No one's indispensable. If you'd been rushed into hospital you'd not be shearing. Come to think of it, if you'd turned up your toes altogether, those sheep would still have been shorn. You're resilient and at the moment you seem pretty good, but you could still get delayed shock or a chill from hours on a stone floor. Be thankful you have a whole bevy of nurses to wait on you. Few have it as good.'

Broderic fumed for a while, then gave up. His last disgruntled remark was to Kate. 'Can't think why you're wearing your uniform. You're my sister and this isn't a hospital. It's daft.'

Kate said calmly, 'It's pyschological. If I wear this it will give me authority. Also, if your friends stay too long, they'll take more kindly to me turning them out—they'll remember my standing too. In your weakened state you'll find a little company goes a long way.'

At that moment the twins arrived. Both had their light brown hair tied in little bunches by their ears, Louise's with blue ribbon, Lauris's with gold. They looked sweet, even angelic, and Lauris wore brown denims with a bright gold top and Louise's blue jeans were stitched with scarlet and she had a red top. They advanced demurely. 'Mother said we could come and look at you and see how much better you are this morning. She did so, Jane.'

Jane said mildly, 'I wasn't going to doubt you. Mr Adair will realise he has to put up with being Exhibit A in the startling case of the missing runholder, especially by the party who found him. You nearly scared seven bells out of my little sisters, Mr Adair.'

Kate said, 'For goodness' sake, aren't you on first name terms yet? Can't imagine Esmeralda allowing that!'

Jane grinned a little. 'Things are rather different now.'

Broderic Adair would get her meaning. But he merely grinned and said, 'Back to Rory or Broderic, Jane. Having plucked your adversary from the jaws of death, you can't go on being formal.'

'Adversary?' The three of them echoed that. 'What can you mean?'

His voice was derisive. 'Jane knows. We fought on sight. Don't let it worry you, we both like fighting.'

Kate's voice was dry too. 'That doesn't make for formality as a rule. Girls, I think Rory should make a speech of thanks to you two. How come you found him? He could still have been lying in that barn while we had search-parties up Cruachan and Bruach.'

'We went in for wheat to feed those chooks. That part was in shadow. It was all spooky and darkish ... and suddenly we saw a—*a shape*! It was a terrible moment, wasn't it, Lou?'

'Sure was. We were absolutely rooted to the floor—I never knew what that meant till then. I felt my blood run cold. I'll never forget it.'

'Then the sun shone in a bit more and we could see the figure was lying very still. We called out, "Who are you?" and "What's wrong there?" but there was no answer and we felt terrified.'

'What exactly did you see?' asked Rory, interestedly.

'We saw a man, lying awkwardly, with an arm all lying funny. The ladder, or bits of it, were lying across him and his face was covered with blood. Your face. It looked as if it had bled a lot and for a long time, and you were so still. It was gruey and——'

Jane said, 'That's enough clinical details, thank you. Then you turned and belted for home and Mother?'

Lauris's brown eyes were full of indignation. 'We did not! We rushed across, thought he was dead, but said in case he wasn't, but was beyond speaking, "We're just going for help, sir," and tore out.'

'You did magnificently,' said Broderic, 'but for you I might even now be a corpse.'

Kate hooted. 'What, with a dislocated shoulder and a cut on your face? Break it down!'

Broderic said, 'Is there anything more callous than the medical profession? Girls, I can see I'm going to have to retain your services if I'm to be able to exist in the style to which I've been accustomed. There are some things I'd like you to do for me. If I ask my sister she'll say all in good time, and tuck me firmly down. I want you to bring my electric razor from Starlight, it's in the bathroom cabinet. And beside the phone in my office is a pad with a few memos on it. Bring it here and I'll get you to do some ringing for me. You can take it in turns.'

'You can have your razor,' said his sister firmly, 'but talking to them about the phone calls can wait. When you've finished shaving, you're going to have a sedative and a sleep.'

Lauris said, 'You don't think he'd sleep better if he got his business messages away? It could ease his mind.'

Broderic chuckled, then winced. 'I can see these twins know their onions. Kate, I've three messages I must get away, and one is really urgent. Then I'll submit gracefully.'

The twins looked smug. They went away, full of importance, to find ballpoint and pad. Jane knew she ought to be thankful that at least his enmity did not extend to the children. Also that at the moment he was playing it her way till he should be on his feet again, and under no obligation to the girl who stood in the way of his dream of restoring the Starlight property to its former proportions.

She said, 'And now I must get things organised. I want to clean out the Centre thoroughly or Mother will forget she's still convalescent to a certain degree, and attack it with vigour. Tomorrow I'll let the coach companies know we're in business again.' Her look as she went out of his bedroom was eloquent of her determination to succeed.

She had come back up for a window-mop when she heard Louise on the telephone. Her young clear voice carried. 'No, I'm ringing on behalf of Mr Broderic Adair of Starlight Peaks, and my instructions were to speak to Mr Mervington personally. Mr Adair is recovering from a severe fall at the moment.'

Jane stopped dead. For the life of her she couldn't help listening. Mervington was the name of the solicitor who'd written to acquaint her of Esmeralda's legacy.

Louise's voice registered satisfaction. Given other circumstances, Jane would have chuckled at her precise, grown-up tones. 'Ah, Mr Mervington. I'm ringing from Wedgwood House where Mr Broderic Adair is being nursed by my mother. He had a most unfortunate accident yesterday. He crashed from a rickety ladder and dislocated his shoulder and had to have his cheek stitched. But it's not too serious. Um—let me have a look at what he told me to write on this pad ... ah yes, "With reference to the matter he discussed with you recently, he wishes no further steps to be taken in this until he is able to come into your office and conduct the business personally. He was unable to negotiate and is reluctant, at the moment, to pursue the matter further. He also wishes you not to contact the other party involved till he sees you."'

Evidently the solicitor had asked who she was. 'Oh, I'm Louise Eastwood and my twin sister and my older sister and mother are all living at the Wedgwood House. It's ours now.' Suddenly she dropped her grown-up air and said excitedly, *We* found Rory. He'd had the accident in the middle of the afternoon and this was after dinner. It was a ladder to the loft in the barn, you see. But he's in very good hands. My mother is a nurse-aide and his sister arrived last night—I expect you know she's a physiotherapist. I beg your pardon? Yes, I'll go and ask him.'

She sped past Jane into the bedroom, said, 'Mr Mervington said he'd come out here if you wanted this discussion to take place soon.'

Broderic said very firmly, 'No. Tell him on no account to bother to come all this way. I'll see him next week.'

Jane walked back to the Centre in a very thoughtful mood. Last night, in his confused state, Broderic had said Jane had spiked his guns. Had he meant because Esmeralda had left her the house, or the fact that he was a patient in her house and he could hardly try to oust her in any way when he was under an obligation to her? Once he was well, would he try to bring any pressure to bear upon her, to surrender this property to him? Could he?

Jane realised she knew next to nothing of legal matters. If it was just a matter of his offering her a higher price, she could turn it down. But if some agreement had been drawn up when Esmeralda had been allowed to purchase this, something like a lien on the property,-where would she stand? Jane certainly didn't like the fact that Broderic Adair's solicitor had also been Esmeralda's, and now was hers.

Later Kate came down to the Centre with a flask of coffee. She laughed. 'Don't thank me for the hospitality ... the cookies are yours. Your mother is with Rory, so I thought I'd give you a hand down here. This is even more charming than I remember—the pictures will be a great draw. The locals will buy too. It's odd, despite the fact that they see mountains out of every window, their walls are covered with alpine scenes too.

'Jane, it's going to be fun having you here. I know I'll miss the fun of working with a staff, yet I'm itching to get going on doing Starlight up. Mother said that last time she was down, it was beginning to look as if it lacked a woman's hand. Aren't your sisters entertaining? Your mother chased them out in case they made Rory's head worse, but I'm sure he was finding them diverting.'

Jane looked alarmed. 'I told them to report back to him, then skedaddle. They'll get too big for their boots if he treats them like secretarial staff. A good job Mother's there, seeing I'm not, or goodness knows how many family secrets they'd impart. Or how many opinions they'd air.'

Kate giggled. 'Just as well you weren't within earshot. They were telling him what a godsend it was having Wedgwood House left to you.' Jane thought Kate gave her a questioning look at that point but couldn't imagine why. 'They said it was just what was needed to free you of your old-maid complex.' Kate's laughter bubbled up at Jane's outraged expression and her indignant: 'Old maid! Me? I'm only——'

'Oh, they didn't mean in age, they meant in outlook. They said they knew you'd made up your mind to sacrifice yourself on the altar of duty, that you regarded yourself as the breadwinner and mainstay of the family. But now they had a house to live in and their mother's pictures were selling too, you would be free to marry. I'm afraid Rory egged them on. He's like that. He said, "I can well imagine she feels that; at her advanced age, anyway, she's probably given up all hope." But he got his come-uppance then. Lauris flashed round on him and said, "Where did you get that idea? Men simply go down like ninepins before her!" '

Jane gave a moan, said, 'I'll kill them! I'll tear them limb from limb. Neither thing is true. But go on, tell me the worst.'

'They said you were the most sought-after waitress in the

hotel, that you could have taken a position many times as a hostess on island cruises but it would have meant too much time away from your painting; that a wealthy Tasmanian business man had come back three years runing to try to persuade you to marry him, but you'd dedicated your life to supporting the family and turned your back on love!'

Jane clenched her fists. 'The nits! They get carried away. I've only had to support the family since Dad died—a few months, and even then it was shared with Mother. That Tasmanian was twice my age and such a bore! I hope to heaven those brats don't babble like that all round the district. What's got into them? Are they trying to put my stock up? That man never mentioned marriage, that's imagination running riot. He was just like so many men on holiday ... it made him feel no end of a lad to be dancing with a young woman. I'm sure he was a dyed-in-the-wool bachelor who'd have taken off and never stopped running if I'd taken him at all seriously. You know places like that go to some men's heads ... waving palms, flowers in the air, soft music, no reality about it at all.'

Kate said soberly, 'Yes, I've heard it has that effect on some.'

Jane could have bitten her tongue out. She'd been far too indignant about the girls to realise where she was heading. She pulled herself up, said, 'The men probably feel downright embarrassed about it when they get back to everyday life. In fact, it's probably a good experience for them. That sort of thing soon palls and doesn't mean a thing. Kate, those pomanders Esmeralda made are just the sort of thing Mother likes making. The little herb jars too. She's going to love it here. It seems as if this niche was made for her.'

Kate said, 'Do you know, when first I heard Esmeralda was gone and I knew I'd never see her again, I nearly broke my heart. I was a bit low, anyway, I was down with 'flu. I know she was very old, but that doesn't stop me missing her. I had to make myself think that there were compensations in all things, as she herself so often said. So I became thankful she'd been spared any long illness, and was glad that after all these years, Starlight was going to regain its lost acres. But then I began thinking about the way she'd built up her little business here; she'd made a valuable folk-craft contribution to the tourist industry. To shut it down would be a great loss to the travelling public and to the area.

'You may not know it, but her cottage and garden is featuring on this year's scenic calendars, with a little paragraph on how she created beauty out of an old school. I got to thinking about how Rory and his men would never have the time to keep this garden going. I know they'd have made good the scars left by demolishing the building, but it would have gone back. So when I came in last night and found you here . . . and got things sorted out . . . I was glad that after all, there was someone to carry on.'

Jane said bleakly, 'Rory doesn't think so. He'll resent it afresh every time he has to take the stock out on the main highway. I'll always be a thorn in his flesh.'

Kate looked at her curiously. 'He had it in his power not to let Esmeralda live here. My people had bought this place back when the school amalgamated with Athol. The road didn't sweep so close then, and they used to be able to drive the stock through at the back of the shelter-shed. It wasn't on the road then, and buyers had to come up. But when she needed it, Rory let her have it, on the understanding that it would come back to its original purpose some day. He has a heart like butter, you know. It melts at a touch. That's why he wouldn't let them carve up Eyrewell's when they'd just got a start. So don't upset yourself, Jane, he won't look on you as a thorn in the flesh for long.'

Jane was hard put to it not to tell Kate everything. A heart of butter . . . but he wasn't going to let Jane melt it. Why? She thought she knew. Was it because Esmeralda had left her the property, and he thought she had schemed for just that? That she was, after all, tarred with the same brush as her grandfather? The sins of the fathers did indeed get visited upon the children and the children's children . . . but not because God had organised it. No, he was a God of Love, but in a world of logic and order and sequence, it was inevitable. Rory might even think she'd brought pressure upon her godmother to leave her will like that. It must have been very recent.

When Jane didn't reply Kate said, 'Jane, if you look on yourself as a thorn, it could colour your attitude to Rory, and that would be a pity.'

Jane put her duster down, looked up smiling, said, 'Kate, you're a thoroughly nice person. It—it's just that we've known insecurity for so long, I hate to think I'm in any way here on sufferance.'

'You've no need to think that. Rory might have wished at first that things had fallen out differently, but he's so adaptable. I mean, he certainly went the second mile with Esmeralda. Not only letting her have the house, but always doing it up. I don't think she ever suspected how much he did. He gradually renewed all the guttering . . . saying it had been left over from some of the farm repairs; there was always enough paint to freshen it up, and a man with time on his hands. Occasionally when Esmeralda protested when something was too apparent, he'd get her to do his washing for him, instead of Lisel, who'd pretend she was too busy, or he'd get her to help with the baking at shearing-time. So don't feel he begrudges you this. Even if he is my brother, there's nobody like him. Oh, if Rory could hear me he'd tell me my tongue was always hung in the middle! I sometimes wish I was more reserved.'

But there *had* been a time when Kate had become reserved, when she'd concealed her feelings, when she'd given Scott up without having it out with him. Jane surprised Kate by putting an arm round her and hugging her. 'Kate, never be anything but yourself. Being reserved causes more trouble than enough. Someone once said, I forget who, that silence can cause more harm than speech; it can too. The times people's love-affairs have got into a snarl simply because one of them was too proud to ask for an explanation! In marriage too, reserve can build up a whole wall of misunderstanding. Hark at me! You'd think I'd had half a dozen marriages in my past, or been a counsellor. I've got to confess I heard our minister in Suva say just that. My tongue must be hung in the middle too.'

Then she dropped all her cleaning things with a great clatter so that Kate wouldn't wonder why she'd said just that. It served as a diversion, but she hoped that later Kate's mind would return to it, ponder it, wonder if, after all, she ought not to have tackled Scott on the subject. Being engaged surely gave one the right to demand an explanation.

She was pondering something herself. What *had* Broderic meant when he asked had Kate recognised her? And that bit about the photo. What did that mean? He'd said, too, he hadn't wanted 'you two to meet', what on earth could one make of that?

Jane had an idea. Perhaps he'd meant he didn't want Kate and Scott to meet yet. Perhaps he wanted to talk to Kate first. That could be it—after all, he had had a nasty crack on the head. Kate seemed to have accepted it as that.

'Well, Kate, let's call it a day. We'll go on up and get lunch now. Mother may have started it if your brother is asleep.'

They came up to the house to find their lunch set out on the kitchen table and Willy assisting Broderic Adair with his. 'It's harder than one realises,' he complained, 'to manage food with just one hand.'

Willy said, 'I'll make you a Madras curry for dinner. You can just fork that up and not feel so helpless. Oh, Jane, that solicitor phoned you. He said you were probably very busy settling in, as well as nursing Rory, and not to worry if you don't see him for a few weeks. There was nothing urgent.'

'Oh, good. Because I don't aim to go further than the village for some time. I want you to get out in the garden, Mother, and get some watercolours done of the various charming corners. They'll sell well.'

'And in no time you ought to be shot of me,' said Broderic. 'I'm a complication, but as soon as the doctor allows it, I'll be back at Starlight.'

Willy had picked up his tray and taken it out and Kate had followed her. Jane waited till they were out of earshot and said, 'It sticks in your crop, doesn't it, Broderic Adair, to have to be grateful to the people who are keeping you out of this property? Don't set up any complexes. I can stand your presence here if you can stand it yourself. My mother would be horrified if she thought that I didn't appreciate having you under our roof. And I won't have her disturbed in any way, let me tell you that.'

'Then, seeing you're so protective towards your mother, you ought to be able to understand my attitude towards Kate.'

Jane was surprised. 'Oh, are you harking back to that? I don't think you rate much on the psychological approach. Kate is tougher than you think. She'll probably realise pride doesn't get you very far and tax Scott outright before long, and she'll more than likely find there was nothing in it. Not enough to break an engagement for, anyway.'

'You still adhere to that?' he demanded.

'Yes. I don't think Scott Mackenzie was serious about anyone save Kate.'

The grooves in his cheeks deepened, the hazel eyes narrowed. 'You interest me, Jane Grey, you interest me very much.'

It puzzled her. She didn't answer. He said, 'You'd like me to believe there was nothing in it, wouldn't you?'

'Of course. It would iron things out, wouldn't it?'

'What if I told you I got complete proof that he certainly did play round with another girl while he was out there?'

Jane knew her cheeks warmed with temper, but she subdued it. She said quietly, 'Then why tantalise me now? If you want to say you told me you thought there was more to it than I could believe, just say so. I don't mind being in the wrong. I'll have to accept it, if what you say is beyond doubt, only I'm sorry. Because having met Kate, I can just imagine what a lovely couple they'd make.' Something struck her. 'How on earth, at this distance from Fiji, could you get proof?'

His look was piercing. For some reason it was beginning to make her feel uncomfortable. He said, 'Well, they say the camera doesn't lie. I flew up to see this girl who told Kate. I expect her motives were good, though I could still choke her. She showed me photos taken of Scott and this other girl. There was no doubt.'

Jane said, 'You can't mean compromising photos? Good heavens, this is beginning to sound like a sordid report from a private investigator specialising in divorce! I can't believe that of——'

'Oh, not lushly so. Merely affectionate, shall we say?'

'But—but if they permitted these photos to be taken, surely there can't be much in them? I mean, you know what these high-spirited holiday groups are like ... they get together, drape arms about each other, fool about in the most innocuous way. Surely——'

'Oh, it wasn't as innocuous as all that, and the photos were snapped of them unaware.'

Jane felt nauseated. 'I'll just borrow a snappy saying and say that if Kate has friends like that, she doesn't need enemies. I think it was low to sneak round like that.'

She walked out of the room.

CHAPTER NINE

WITH shearers descending upon them, Broderic fretting meanwhile like a caged lion, and knowing the rush and bustle of Christmas preparation would follow immediately upon their departure, there wasn't much time for dwelling on emotional problems and their solutions; it was just a case of wondering, as each day dawned, how to cope with all that must be done.

Broderic Adair went down to Queenstown for his X-rays, Hamish driving him. The solicitor rang Jane one day, said he realised how busy she must be, that he himself was flat out getting all sorts of business up to date before Christmas and was leaving for a North Island holiday immediately after. He suggested they left things as they were till the holiday season was over, and forwarded her an advance from Esmeralda's small savings bank account. Jane knew relief. There was evidently going to be no trouble from that quarter. Their care for Broderic Adair had scotched any move he might have made against them. It would have been embarrassing to turn round and bite the hands that had smoothed his unconscious brow, she supposed. Even so, she had a feeling that he would just bide his time and in the new year, would make another offer. He would be wasting his time. Business was excellent at the Centre, Mother's pictures were selling as well as Jane's, and she was even spending some time potting now.

They got into a better routine when Broderic was able to return to Starlight. He and Jane had a set-to when he wanted to reimburse them for his and Kate's keep while there.

Red rags of rage flew in her cheeks. 'We may have seemed on our beam-ends, and were openly grateful to Esmeralda for providing us with a solution, but price can't be put upon hospitality. Kate's been an enormous help. She even coped

161

on her own with several sessions at the shop. She's a marvellous saleswoman. I can scarcely rave about my own work, but she does. And she won't take a penny for it, yet you talk about paying. It's an insult!'

'All right. It looks as if I'll have to accept that ... and don't dare tell me I hate being under an obligation to you. I can do a bit of insisting on my own. As soon as shearing's over I'll get the men to kill two or three lambs for you and bag it for your deep freeze.'

Jane snorted. 'That's just another way of paying. It saves your pride. I'm beginning to realise the Adair pride is something to reckon with.'

'Do you? Then you can just stop making those cookies right away, Jane Grey!' She looked at him, startled. He added, 'Now don't argue with me, I know they're for us. I heard you telling Kate that to make up for the hours she had spent at the shop, you were going to do a few batches for the shearers' smoke-ohs. It's got to be a two-way thing. Otherwise, we won't take them.'

They measured glances, then Jane said, 'All right, I'll take the lamb, but for Kate's sake, because she surely does need these.'

He grinned and started for the door, then said, 'So we can part almost amicably for once.'

She ignored that, said, 'Broderic, have you ever told Kate that Scott was here and that I'd met him in Fiji?'

'What do you think? Of course I haven't. It would only upset her.'

'Or would it upset you?'

The hazel eyes flashed. 'What can you mean? Explain yourself.'

'Just that I can't help wondering if you really want Kate and Scott to make it up.'

'What? Why should you think that? Except that if he is a gay deceiver, I wouldn't want that for my sister. And since I saw that photo, I've grave doubts. Apart from that, why would I?'

162

Jane looked at him steadily. 'She's a good housekeeper and you're a bachelor farmer, and Starlight is beautifully looked after again. Every moment Kate could spare, she was up there putting spit and polish on. That's why.'

He looked at her with positive dislike. 'That's below the belt and entirely undeserved.'

She knew it and felt despicable. Words wouldn't come to her. They stuck in her throat. Meanwhile he continued to look at her that way. He said, 'Just imagine, I was exasperated with Esmeralda's lack of discernment when she married your grandfather. But now I know I'm not half as discriminating myself as I thought. I can't trust my judgment any more. I'd never have dreamed during that lull in our hostilities you'd even be capable of a remark like that.'

Jane put down the palette knife she was icing her custard squares with, turned, said miserably, 'I'll have to say sorry. I oughtn't to have said it. I know you'd never try to keep them apart if you felt you could trust Scott; that at least as far as Kate is concerned, you're a good brother.'

To her surprise he came across to the table and said, 'Thanks for apologising. It would have rankled otherwise. Jane, oh, Jane, why can't you be open with me? Why not make a clean breast of things?'

That really did it. 'Open with you? You think I schemed from the time I got here to get Esmeralda to alter her will in my favour! You think if I confess that, you'll have the chance to be forgiving, in your lordly way, and say you understand it, that you can see I was desperate for a home. I can see it all ... that horribly cruel letter, the miserly offer for this house and grounds—you must think I've no idea of New Zealand property values—it was all because you thought it ought to come to you. Looked at fairly and squarely, I suppose it ought to have. It was sheer bad luck for you that Esmeralda came into my exhibition that day, but a godsend for me. My need was far greater than yours. This situation is like Naboth's vineyard all over again. You have this enormous estate and you covet my little flower-patch! I'd no idea Esmeralda would leave it to me. If I'd thought about it at all, I'd have thought that seeing Thomas had some nephews in Australia, it would have gone to them.

'I felt really safe and secure for the first time since Noel died when it was left to me. And let me tell you this, Broderic Adair, you weren't the only one to feel your judgment had let you down. I loved your care of Esmeralda ... but for you she'd have just eked out an existence, I know that. You allowed her to buy this place cheaply, you did it up for her—Kate told me how you used to pretend you had materials over and men looking for a job—I thought we were going to be pretty lucky to have a neighbour like you. Then that letter came. I was bitterly disillusioned.

'Now, it doesn't seem possible to keep away from each other. Your accident threw us together. The children think of you as a brother, Mother has a great affection for you, and Kate just loves to come down here. This is like a family situation, where there is jealousy because one member is left a bigger share. Are you going to wear a chip on your shoulder for the rest of your life because of that?'

His face looked graven, harsh. He seemed to be thinking deeply.

'What if I told you, Jane, that I had never once, through all the years, thought Esmeralda might have left this property to me? What would you say?'

'I wouldn't believe you,' said Jane, and stalked from his presence.

Through the preliminary preparations for Christmas Jane carried a heavy heart. So too, she believed, did Kate. They filled the tins with mince-pies, shortbread, cookies, biscuits, puddings. They helped the twins to do their Christmas shopping in Queenstown, and Jane found compensation in letting them spend more freely than ever before on all the gaudy trifles, the tinsel, the imitation snow, the paper chains, the silver and gold bells, the candles. She was pleased when they spent most of their own money on a beautifully constructed crib, and built their own version of the Stable at Bethlehem round it in the conservatory, of flat stones from the hillside, and ransacked the Adair children's old toybox for model animals to stand inside it. She and Kate had a good chuckle, even if they shooed them out, when they found them sneaking Minto and Pinto in to look at it. Kate said, as the girls led the donkeys away, 'That was sweet, really, symbolic. And donkeys have such wise faces, I could almost believe they carried an ancient memory of that first stable, and it was reflected in their eyes.'

At times Jane wished the two homes had been further distant, or that Louise and Lauris didn't worship Rory so much. He taught them to groom the donkeys, to eye-clip sheep, to dive in the pool that was in constant use now; he was very patient with their determination to set eggs under every broody bantam, even if it wasn't a paying game so late in the season.

When Bernie suggested various methods of turning the bantams off their broodiness, Louise flashed round on him. 'It's monstrous! It's flying in the face of nature! Why should the ones who go clucky early get chickens and the later ones not? It denies their maternal instincts. It's just like some woman thinking she's going to have a baby and then having a miscarriage!' Then, disgustedly, 'What are you guffawing at, Bernie? Anyway, Rory's the boss and he says we can have some of his fertile eggs and that he'll never miss the bit of wheat for their keep even if they're hatched so late they only lay when eggs are plentiful.'

'I give up,' said Bernie, cowering away from her wrath, 'if the chief's in league against me, who am I to protest? But bless my boots, if he's not the biggest softy I ever knew since you two came on the scene. I'm expecting to see the donkeys in sunbonnets and the ducks in galoshes any moment,' and he ran away with the twins in hot pursuit.

Willy watched them from the kitchen window one night, Rory, Bernie and Mick, playing cricket with the twins on the flat area beside the Adair Water.

'He ought to be married, with a family of his own coming along,' she said fondly. 'He's essentially a family man.'

'Bernie?' asked her daughter innocently. 'Oh, I don't know. He's young enough yet.'

'I didn't mean Bernie and well you know it,' said her mother. 'They're calling out for you. Off you go. The exercise will do you good.'

Kate came down from the big house and presently Lisel and Hamish and their family arrived. Jane knew it was pleasant to forget enmity and join in carefree fun like this. Rory wasn't allowed to bat yet, but was an excellent bowler, using his good arm. Jane was hopeless at both batting and bowling, but a great fielder, they told her. She was in white shorts and top, and the cool air off the mountain tops was balm and refreshment after the heat and burden of the day.

All about them the scents of the garden drifted; the resinous pines added their own tang and from every cleft on Bruach the wild thyme flung its own pungency. These long twilit evenings, lasting now till after ten o'clock, were heavenly. If it hadn't been for the distrust, or dislike, or whatever it was Rory had for her, and the sad cast of Kate's features in repose, this would indeed have been Eden.

The rest of the Adair clan accepted Jane with a friendliness that knew no resentment. Uncle Robert Adair and Aunt Stella told the twins to call them just that. They and Lucinda and Giles and their adorable Kenneth, with Mhairi and Fergus and their parents, often came over and always called in at the Wedgwood House too, linking both houses as had always been the custom.

At last they'd had enough. Willy called from the open window, 'Come on up to the patio, I'm bringing out cool drinks. I've given up working.'

Kate and Jane looked at each other, and with but one thought in their minds raced for the privilege of occupying the garden swing before the twins could beat them to it.

Jane said, as they flung themselves on it and set it in motion with their sandalled feet on the flags, 'Kate, you're looking particularly beautiful tonight ... those yellow shorts look gorgeous against your long tanned legs ... and that top with the yellow roses sprinkled over the brown background looks so summery. I wish I'd an apricot skin like yours, you never sunburn. Yet so many people with chestnut hair do. Ever since you came here I've had a yen to do portraits. If I could, I'd paint you against the afterglow and call it, "The Sunset Girl". Wonder if I've got the confidence to try?'

Kate said, 'Are you ever lacking in confidence, Jane? I feel you even give people like me a certain sureness of themselves.'

Jane said soberly, 'I think we all put up a certain façade, Kate, but are aware of things we lack. Even the ones who appear extroverts, careless and gay, are often just covering up.'

The others reached them and conversation became general. Willy came out with a huge pitcher of her own delectable brand of summer drinks, a mixture of pineapple and grapefruit juice, laced with ginger ale. The cool sound of ice tinkling against its green frosted sides stimulated the gastric juices, Broderic said.

While Willy was serving the others who'd cast themselves down on various garden seats, Jane, as they swung, said to Kate in a low tone, 'You've the most perfect profile ... those loops of yellow nylon ribbon tying your hair back up high make you look like something in the eighteenth century, so why do you——'

Kate's silver laughter floated out on the clear air. 'Jane, you goose! Imagine women in shorts in the eighteenth century! It'd have to be hooped skirts and fichus.'

'I mean it, from the chin up ... pure eighteenth century, the age of romance. Kate, why do you have an inferiority complex?'

The laughter stilled. Kate's tone was bitter. 'Because someone I loved let me down. It destroyed all my confidence. I just can't seem to get it back, though you've helped.'

The others, unknowing, drew them into general conversation. Kate said, having a refill, 'Even the fact that those ice-blocks are made from spring water gives this concoction a taste unequalled anywhere. The purity of it! Our minister in Palmerston spoke of David thirsting for water from the well of Bethlehem once, and I knew exactly what he meant. I longed for a glass of ours.'

Broderic said, 'We're so fortunate. I had a trip to Singapore once and the sight of those immense blocks of flats really got to me—no contact at all with the good earth, day after day. No grass for hot little feet, no pure springs bubbling out of deep mountains, as fresh as dew. Those children, I thought, have only one life to live, as have we all, and never to have known these things is indeed a tragedy. Contact with Mother Earth ought to be an essential ingredient of every childhood.'

At moments like these, Jane knew a longing that was almost unbearable ... he was so kindred ... a longing for all the enmity to be swept away. Into the stillness of the evening came the sound of a car.

Broderic groaned. 'Oh, no, not visitors! I'm not in the mood.'

Jane was higher up than he was and looked over her shoulder. 'Only one visitor. Some man.'

Not *some* man ... it was Scott Mackenzie! She heard Kate give a betraying gasp. Then Scott, ignoring Kate ... had he seen her? ... said, 'Hullo, Jane. I said I'd be back. Hullo, Willy, that looks good. Hope it's what you used to serve in Fiji. Any left for a jaded traveller? Hi, Rory, Louise, Lauris. Heavens, you girls have grown since you came to New Zealand. Hullo, Kate. I thought I recognised your laugh. I was parking the car. Down for Christmas, are you?'

Kate didn't answer directly. Jane had an idea that Kate would have preferred him to think she was here only temporarily, not even to guess she'd left Palmerston to be away from there when he returned. She dare not lie, though, with the outspoken twins there. Instead she said evasively, 'Well, it's nice to be home for the festive season, but I'm helping Rory out meanwhile.'

Scott took a chair close to the swing after he'd greeted the others. He sipped gratefully. 'I had the sun full on me all the way from Invercargill, till it dipped. It was very lovely but uncomfortably hot. Bit late for a call, but I couldn't resist it. I'm doing right from Queenstown through to North Otago, but will be back this way later. I'm to stay in this area most of January.'

Kate said, her voice cold, 'Surely you won't be doing business in January. You always took your holidays then.'

He sounded bright. 'It will be on holiday. I've got to know a farming family beyond Athol very well, so they've invited me to spend my leave there—sort of busman's holiday. I'm to share in the work of the farm so that Roy can have time off for tramping with me. We're hoping to get into that Never-never country back of Lake Wakatipu. We can get access through the mountains at the back of his place.'

Jane saw Kate's hands clench on her lap as they swung to and fro. She said quickly, as no one else had answered and Scott might easily feel unwelcome, 'What a splendid time you'll have.'

He nodded. 'Rather. That's my type of holiday, much more so than that sophisticated cruise I had to take last year, with all apologies to you and Willy, Jane.'

Jane felt, rather than saw, Kate jerk to look sideways at her. She kept her voice very casual. 'Well, it wasn't what you'd have chosen, but it did wonders for your sister, didn't it? She needed all that gay company. It was wonderful how she joined in everything eventually.'

Scott said quite affectionately, with a look in Willy's direction, 'Well, that was due in the main to your mother. When I went off on that island trip, Jill realised she *could* mix again without Greg at her side to look after her. The island trip, even though it was still with a group, compensated me a bit—seeing it was more adventurous—for not being down here among mountains.' He hesitated, then added meaningly, 'Or so I thought then. But it was certainly a mistake not coming here.'

No one replied. Lisel whispered something to Hamish. Sholto was fast asleep on her lap and she thought they ought to go home now. Bernie and Mick decided to call it a day too. Willy said, 'Lauris, Louise, you must go to bed now or I'll never get you up in the morning. Don't you others disturb yourselves. I'll see them off.'

Jane found her heart racing. Kate and Scott were here together, but not alone. She mustn't be too pointed about it, but if she could wangle Broderic away, she would. There was a silence after the good-nights faded on the still mountain air. Jane sensed by Kate's stiffness that she'd like to get up and flee, but felt that it might be better to pretend an indifference.

Scott said, in a purely conversational tone, 'I've had the most enjoyable time down here. It was to be just a fill-in, but now I'm told that when my three months is up I can have this area if I wish.'

Jane had to reply. 'How marvellous for you, when you love mountainous country. Would your base be Invercargill, as now?'

'It wouldn't have to be. I can make it where I like. I thought of Wanaka. I love that lake, and I'm looking round already for a house there. But I'm told it will be easier after Christmas.'

'Wanaka is so dreamy a lake. You'll do all that farming area, I suppose, Hawea, Tarras, the lot?'

'Yes, and right through to Omarama and Benmore. It's the most attractive territory I've ever had.'

Good for Scott. He was letting Kate know he would be in the vicinity of the place she loved most. Jane began to enjoy herself. She'd help things along. But how?

Scott must still have the idea that Kate resented his having given up his holiday with her, to his sister. He said,

'Main thing about being in the North Island, of course, was that my folk are up there, but Mother and Dad have always believed in young people learning to stand on their own feet, and they told me if this was offered to me I wasn't to hesitate on their account.'

Kate managed to bring herself to join in. 'How are they, Scott? Did they enjoy their trip to Britain?'

'Yes, very much. Even though they'd been away from there since their schooldays, they renewed friendships very easily and visited all their old haunts. Oddly enough, they came from neighbouring counties. If Jill hadn't improved, they wouldn't have gone. She told them she was fine again and positively pushed them off. Now she's back teaching and loving it.'

Nevertheless, it was a strain keeping the conversation going, and Jane felt she was going to face some searching questions from Kate later, as to whether she'd known when he'd called before that he and Kate had once been engaged. Oh, dear! If only she could think how to fade out, taking Broderic with her. But he seemed determined to sit Scott out, with some idea, she supposed, of protecting Kate.

When Willy turned the outside light on for them from inside, Scott said, 'Well, I must get going. Kate, like to walk down to the car with me?'

Jane found herself thinking: 'Oh, do, Kate, do. Give him a chance ... on a night like this, a moon rising, starlit, with all the fragrances of the garden, with the trees whispering secrets and the Adair Water singing on its way, anything could happen.' But Kate said in an indifferent tone, smothering an ostentatious yawn, 'No, I think I'd better go up home, I've a big day tomorrow.'

Jane bridged the gap. 'Are you staying at the Frankton Motor Hotel tonight?'

Scott said quickly, 'Why, if I hadn't booked, would you ask me to spend the night at Wedgwood House again?' (Cunning hound ... what a wonderful opportunity to keep within range of Kate).

'Sure would. Mother would be delighted. But weren't you taking a risk at this time of year, not booking? The tourist season is hotting up now.'

He grinned brazenly. 'I was counting on your reputation for hospitality. I thought you'd never get round to it. When your mother disappeared with the girls I thought I'd have to ask you straight out if you'd put me up. A poor show indeed!'

Kate lost her sleepy air and stared at him. 'What a nerve! Jane and her mother lead very busy lives. Or they might have had a full house with guests of their own.'

He was quite unperturbed. 'Well, surely, despite past relationships, *you'd* have put me up?'

Kate, assuming this would be double Dutch to Jane, said, 'Sorry about this, Jane. The fact is, Scott and I were once engaged, but we—we terminated our engagement.'

'Tidy way of putting it,' said Scott, 'but the real truth of the matter is, you ditched me. Don't embark on explanations, Kate, Jane knows all about it. We had a long talk about it when I stayed here last time. Not to worry, Kate, it's all in the past, and despite the fact that you seem to think we ought therefore to have no dealings with each other ever, I still think I'll call in to see Jane and Willy whenever I feel like it.' He grinned at them unrepentantly.

Jane felt at a loss, but rallied and said, 'Scott, you're just being provocative and Kate's had a long, hot, hard day. I think I'll take you away.'

'A *very* good idea,' drawled Broderic Adair, 'and Scott, if my sister wants it that way, you aren't to bother her.'

Scott said, 'Kate's not a chicken, she can fend for herself. If *she* doesn't mind hurting people, and striking the first blow, then she's got to expect retaliation.'

Kate stood up. 'Come on, Rory, Scott's right in that at least. I *can* fight my own battles, only I thought this particular one was over. And Scott, don't, don't dare try to set Jane and myself at odds. We're the best of pals. This isn't fair to her. She's probably terrified I'm offended she didn't tell me she knew you—and about us. Well, I'm not. Leave her out of it, Scott. It's nothing to do with her!'

Broderic's voice was so dry it almost rasped. 'Isn't it?' he asked, and led Kate away without even a goodnight.

Puzzling over what Broderic could have meant robbed Jane of an hour's sleep, then she told herself to stop trying to fathom it. He was a most unpredictable man. It wasn't her fault Scott was coming here, it was Kate he wanted to see. For all his banter tonight, she sensed he was desperately lonely, missing Kate horribly. Jane knew a fierce pang. Oh, if only Broderic Adair wanted *her* like that, she'd accept *any* overture. Jane sat up in bed, thumped her pillow, said, 'You idiot! Who'd want to marry an enigmatical, moody, impossible fellow like that!' She felt much better and fell asleep instantly.

Broderic didn't come near her next day, but Kate did ... after she'd seen Scott take the road to Queenstown. She had shadows under her eyes, but didn't seem in a reserved mood.

She said, 'Sorry you got involved in that last night, Jane. It's hardly fair to you. And Rory's taking up such a stupid attitude towards it—seems to be blaming you for Scott being here.' She stopped, said, 'Jane! I think he's jealous of Scott and you. Could it be?'

Jane's surprise was genuine. 'It couldn't possibly be that. For one thing, to be brutally candid, your brother went to great lengths to keep me out here. That doesn't add up to attraction. For another, there'd be no reason whatsoever, even if he fancied me himself, to be jealous of Scott.' She hesitated and plunged. 'Kate, I think Scott's heart is entirely yours. He told us in Fiji that he was engaged to a super girl. He didn't tell us your name, and I never dreamed I'd meet you. So when——'

Kate said sharply, 'Don't hesitate, out with it. So when——?'

'So when he came here that first time, it was to see Rory,

173

to ask about you. I had a feeling he couldn't help coming. He was most surprised to see me. He and Rory had a short session and didn't seem to get anywhere. Scott was restless and wanted to walk it off, so I went with him and he told me he'd been engaged to you.' (She mustn't let on that Rory had told her what had happened).

'I didn't let on I knew when we first met, Kate, I thought it was entirely your own affair. But Scott told me that he just couldn't believe you two wouldn't be spending the rest of your lives together. He wondered if you might have thought he would always put his family first, because of taking his sister to Fiji. Did you feel that, Kate?' (This might jolt Kate into saying why she'd broken it off).

Kate looked insulted. 'Oh, no, Jane. I thought it was tremendous of Scott to do just that. I'm not in the least possessive. There are so many relationships in life. The husband and wife one has to be the closest, the dearest, but I'd never expect to own a man. Those sort of relationships burn up out of their very intensity. It just doesn't work. Besides, Scott asked me to go too. I said no, that I wanted a holiday down home, but my real reason was that I felt it would do Jill good to have her brother to herself. Scott and I were so much in love, and I was afraid Jill might feel the odd man out, the unwanted third. I didn't tell Scott that in case he told Jill. But as things turned out, I should have gone.'

'Why?'

Kate didn't hesitate. 'Because Scott fell for someone else over there. I heard he really played around, had a ball of a time. I wouldn't want a husband I couldn't trust to go off on a holiday alone, so I gave him up. It saved my pride to keep my reason to myself. I thought it would jolly well serve him right to wonder why, might make him less cocksure. He's too handsome by far, you know. I'd much rather have an ugly man.'

A chuckle escaped Jane. 'Oh, Kate, Kate! You don't want anyone *but* Scott. Look, I'm suspicious about this. Because his sister needed a bit of extra attention, I saw more of Scott than I did of some guests, and his behaviour was exemplary. For instance, when he said he was engaged it was in front of the whole tour group. How did you hear, and what was said?'

'It was from a girl I went to school with. She's up north now too. She seemed very concerned for me. She cried when she told me.'

Jane scowled. 'Haven't you heard of crocodile tears? Was she a friend you could trust . . . absolutely?'

Kate hesitated. 'I wasn't very fond of her at school. Oh, it sounds so petty after all these years, and kids are sometimes like that and get over it. I beat her once or twice in school sports. She seemed very jealous. It was silly, because in other events I wasn't even placed, but she seemed to have improved.'

Jane was sceptical. 'Did she know Scott before this cruise?'

'No, she'd heard I was engaged and was quite surprised when he told her his fiancée's name.'

'Ah, now we're getting somewhere. Tell me, what did she say when she told you that bit?'

Kate shrugged, 'Oh, she said, "I thought—well, fancy old Kate snaffling a handsome guy like this." Then she said that was the trouble, other girls always chased the good-lookers.'

Jane's voice held asperity. 'And you, being the possessor of a mighty big inferiority complex, fell for that! I wouldn't be surprised if she tried to make up to Scott and failed. Unattached males can have a helluva time on a cruise. I've seen it happen time and time again. Some of this group were in another guesthouse, I know, but they were often all together, and I never saw Scott make up to any of them. I wonder if I met this so-called friend of yours. Oh, Kate, it wouldn't have been Vanda Shere, would it? She was a pain in the neck to everyone.'

Kate said cautiously, 'It was, but——'

175

'Then it's a lot of old rubbish! I can truly stand as alibi for Scott now. There wasn't anyone else. This was sheer green-eyed jealousy. She did try to pester him, but he really shook her off—stayed with the crowd, danced attendance on Jill. It gave him a good excuse. Vanda pouted about it. I remember she was quite peeved when he suddenly took off on that island trip. Come to think of it, two of the girls who went on that trip were engaged to men in the party, there were two married couples, and the only unattached female was nearly fifty and a widow, a truly good sport. I remember when she came back she said what a pleasant young man Scott was, and she envied his fiancée. Kate, you've just got to see Scott pronto!'

Kate's eyes had lost their adamant look. 'Jane, I'm scared to hope, but that could be true. Oh, dear, my pride got in the way. I—I mustn't make up my mind that's the way it was, but I will tell him why I gave him up. He'll be furious, but I don't care. You're right, he ought to be told the truth. In any case, even if there had been some attraction, it hasn't lasted, has it?'

'I doubt if there was anything to last. I'm sure Scott offered to take this post here because he heard you were coming back to the homestead somehow. Kate, you won't renege on this, will you? Now's not the time for second thoughts. And I'll tell you this, my girl, *if you don't tell Scott, I will*. Kate, get away up home, put your best bib and tucker on and I'll try to trace Scott.'

'Trace him? Isn't he at Frankton?'

'No, I asked where he'd be staying and he said he wasn't sure where he'd be. He had someone to see in Queenstown, a lot round the Arrow basin and Lake Hayes. Oh, I wonder if he'll book in at Drumlogie? I know he stayed there once before, Lucinda told me. She rang one day and said a Scott Mackenzie was staying there and would I tell her if that could be the Scott Mackenzie you'd been engaged to, and if he was, how could Kate let a man like that slip through her fingers?

'I've got to ring her anyway. She's a friend of someone I knew in Fiji, who's now married to a farmer near Roxburgh, Anna Doig. She and Calum are staying at Drumlogie for a day or two and Lucinda said she'd like to bring them over to see our slides of Fiji. Kate, promise me one thing ... you won't get cold feet, will you, if we can't get hold of him immediately?'

Kate said, 'I promise. Seeing him the other night turned my life upside down again. I've been stupid. But I'm not telling Rory. I can't understand his present attitude—when I first broke it off, he was all for a reconciliation, but not now.'

Jane thought that was odd too.

Kate said, 'I'll stand on my own feet like Scott said I should. I'll be frank and to hell with my pride. Jane darling, get on with the ringing. I'd do it myself, but if he was there and Lucinda called him to the phone before I could explain, I couldn't bear it, not with miles of distance between us. When I come out with this I want it to be face to face.'

Jane knew it was going to be all right now. Kate stood there, holding her breath. It was wonderful, Lucinda said. 'Scott rang from Arrowtown less than an hour ago to book in. Can I give him a message? He'll be here just after five. We're full at the house, but I've offered him one of the motels.'

Jane said, 'Lucinda, he was here last night and because of that, Kate wants to see him. The motel would be ideal because they'd have such privacy. Here they wouldn't.' She turned to Kate. 'He'll be in at five, and will have his meal at six. What time would you like to see him?'

Kate lost all her colour at the very thought but said sturdily, 'Seven. If it's not convenient to him, ask him to ring you, not me, to pass the message on.'

Jane said, 'You goat ... he'd skip an appointment with the Governor-General at a message from you! ... Lucinda, tell him seven o'clock. Kate will drive over.'

Lucinda said, 'I was going to ring you later myself—

177

Anna and Calum aren't staying as long as we hoped. Any chance of us coming over for that slide-showing tonight? Be a good idea anyway, as then Kate and Scott wouldn't feel they had to call on us.'

Jane had stars in her eyes as she turned round. Kate said shakily, 'Oh, Jane, don't look like that. It mightn't come off. Oh, Jane, I'm scared!'

Jane said stoutly, 'I'm not. I feel in my bones Vanda lied. Kate, praise the saints the only bus-load for today has been and gone. When you've had a shower I'll set your hair; have it down here. Seeing you don't want to tell Rory, I'll go up to Starlight and get what you want to wear. I'll fob off any questions.'

'Oh, he won't be in. They're away up to the Giant's Causeway. I can't run into them. Come on up with me; I'll pop a casserole in for them, and scrub potatoes to put round it, and they can have fruit and ice-cream for dessert. I'll leave a note saying I've had to go to Queenstown and won't be back till late.'

As they went up Jane said, 'They've been up there a lot lately. Why? They seemed to have stock agents up there the other day, but there's no stock up there.'

'Not stock agents, surveyors. That causeway ends in a solid buttress of rock, you know. They think it could be blasted away, and then Starlight would have access once more to that fifty-acres.'

'Won't it cost the earth?'

'Expensive enough, but they'd save it in a few years in man-power.' Kate looked at Jane sharply. 'Rory isn't making a fuss about having to do it. Don't feel that.'

Jane said a little bleakly, 'Sometimes I wish we hadn't had to accept Esmeralda's legacy. It created such a problem.'

Kate said, 'But it brought compensations. You're such a lovely family to have as neighbours. Rory would have missed old Esmeralda more if it wasn't for your mother and the twins, and you.'

Jane said, 'But I know for certain he'd rather we hadn't come.'

Kate said impulsively, 'But if he'd wanted that, he could have stopped you.' Then she clapped hands to her mouth.

Jane stopped dead in her tracks. 'What can you mean, Kate?'

'Oh, dear, forget I said that. Rory'd kill me if he knew.'

'Knew what?' insisted Jane. 'I must know. Do you mean there was some clause—some option—that could have prevented me?'

She thought Kate looked a little relieved. 'Yes, that was it, but for heaven's sake, don't give me away to my brother. So, Jane, he doesn't resent you as much as you think, or he'd have pushed for what he was promised.'

Jane didn't know what to make of it, but Kate's needs came first today. They put the casserole in, wrote the note, picked out a sleeveless dacron dress in gold for Kate. It had white spots all over it, white binding at neck and armholes. She had yellow patent shoes to go with it, and Jane determined she would wear a hair-clasp of hers that was just a row of yellow daisies, to keep the built-up locks of chestnut hair in place. Jane was going to sweep them up from that slanting fringe.

Back at Wedgwood they worked swiftly, glad that everyone else was visiting the Eyrewells. The dress had a tie of cinnamon gauze that fell to the hem, and Kate wore a chunky Fijian bracelet in brown clasped about her wrist. 'Borrowed plumes,' said Kate, looking at it as she kissed Jane goodbye and got into her car.

Jane watched her go with a prayer in her heart that not a wrong word would be uttered, that no hurt feelings or resentments would be allowed to rise up, and went inside to prepare the evening meal and change the flowers ready for tonight's guests.

CHAPTER TEN

JANE was surprised to see Bernie, Mick, and Broderic coming down at quarter to eight, freshly tubbed, tanned with the summer sun; Broderic in tussore-coloured shorts, and a shirt to match with a tan cravat looped at his throat. He said as he came in, 'The twins invited us, they said the Logies and the Doigs were coming. By the way, where's Kate gone?'

Jane saw the crowd coming in the front door and knew he couldn't set her back in front of them, so said, 'She's gone to Drumlogie. Scott's staying there, you see, in a motel, which will give them maximum privacy. I persuaded her to tell him why she broke it off. Oh, take that look off your face, I didn't break your confidence—she told me the whole thing herself! When she mentioned the name of this supposed friend who told her, I knew it for lies, engendered by sheer jealousy. Vanda Shere made a dead set at Scott, to no avail, bless him. I'm sure Scott never once was disloyal to Kate.'

For once Broderic looked completely at a loss. But he could say nothing, because the visitors were now upon them. Lucinda made an excuse to get Jane to herself, and they went off to Jane's studio. They chatted excitedly about what was happening right now at Drumlogie. Lucinda said, 'I felt like locking them in till they came to their senses. What could they have parted over?' Jane told her. It couldn't matter now.

Giles came in. 'What are you two up to? Rory's suspicious too. I mean to say, Lucinda got our affairs into enough of a snarl to make me wonder if she's the one to try to help untangle somebody else's.'

Lucinda looked indignant. 'I got? Let me tell you, Giles, quarrels are like babies ... it takes two to make them!'

Giles said, 'Lucinda! For the daughter of missionaries, you take the biscuit. How coarse!'

Lucinda giggled, 'I just love shocking Giles. Darling, you and Rory are going to have to eat your words before many hours have passed. You and he are both too hamfisted to do anything constructive about this. Anyway, it's a change to have the pair of you talking about anything but farming when you get together.'

'Oh, we've done that too. He's just told me he's going to blast the blind end of the Giant's Causeway out of existence. He ought to have done that when first the road went through. Then he might have been allowed the use of their machinery to bulldoze a track out, in lieu of some of the compensation they paid him for losing so much frontage on the Wedgwood property.'

Jane gazed at him, mouth open. 'Compensation on the Wedgwood property? You mean on Starlight, don't you?'

Giles gazed at her, puzzled in his turn. 'Same thing, isn't it? It's all one. He owns the lot. But you must know that, seeing you rent this place from him, surely?'

Jane felt the blood leave her face. 'Rent it? I thought I owned it. Esmeralda left me all she owned. Wasn't that the property too?'

Lucinda stood as if turned to stone, and she looked daggers at Giles when she recovered. Giles looked horribly uncomfortable as he realised what had happened. Then he said, 'Oh, I get it! Rory felt you were such bricks, starting a venture like this, and expecting to live with Esmeralda for long enough, he cooked this up. He and Esmeralda shared a solicitor, didn't they? The cunning old fox! Jane, for pity's sake, don't tell Rory I blew it. He's always been that way, he likes to hide his light under the proverbial bushel. Don't spoil a grand gesture like that—oh, lord, here he comes. Jane, don't ...'

Broderic was calling as he came. 'I've got the projector and screen set up. Come on!'

Jane pulled herself together, though the blood was

181

pounding in her ears. 'Don't draw the blinds yet, Broderic, Mother's got coffee and sandwiches to serve first. We'll have drinks at the interval. I've planned quite a do.'

Anna and Jane had a lot to talk about, but finally the show got under way. The slides were magnificent. They showed all facets of Fijian life.

The twins and Anna filled in a lot of the commentary, with the former providing quite a few laughs in their candid comments. Jane was glad of this, for it was taking her all her time to concentrate. The property wasn't theirs. *It had never been theirs.* Yet Broderic had been generous enough to offer her a few thousands for it! And she had actually twitted him with being miserly! No wonder he hadn't wanted them here. She couldn't think it all out. She must appear normal before her guests. Giles was working the projector, and Jane kept on talking as each slide appeared on the screen. Remorse and confusion were washing over her in waves.

There was the sound of a door quietly opening. Broderic said, 'Who's that?'

Scott's voice answered. It carried a wealth of meaning in its very confidence. 'Just Kate and me. Carry on, folks. Kate and I will be quite happy to just sit at the back and hold hands. We're engaged again.'

That did it! Lucinda sprang at the switch and flooded the room with light. Lauris's young voice was heard to say, 'I don't know what they mean, engaged *again!*'

Scott was laughing, so was Kate. She said bravely, 'Someone made mischief, but Jane sorted it out. She didn't believe it could possibly be true, so she sent me off to Scott to tell him my true reasons for giving him up. And it was all lies. Vanda has been found out.'

It was at that moment that Jane saw Broderic's expression. Unlike the rest he wasn't looking at the happy pair. He was looking at Jane, and she couldn't have read his look, except that it wasn't gladness. He looked dazed, nothing more. He recovered himself, then added his good wishes.

As they went to seat themselves again, he passed very close to Jane, said in a low but intense tone, 'We must have a talk about this, I don't care how late. You and I both know it isn't—wasn't—lies!'

Jane was glad to sit down. Her knees felt like cotton wool. This was one shock on top of the other! Now for the balance of these slides. The twins settled themselves on cushions at her feet, and as she came to the end, they expressed disappointment. 'We thought you were going to show the ones of the musical. *We* were in that.'

Well, at least it was going to postpone the talk with Broderic. Jane took them out and said, 'Well, Kate would be very interested too. Scott features in some. We put it on outdoors, on the beach. It saved a lot of backdrop scenery. The palms and hibiscus flowers were there, ready. It was great fun, except that the leading man broke a leg and Scott was pressganged into taking the part. It so happened he knew all the songs. We were very lucky in having a guest with such a fine tenor voice.'

Scott, from the back, chuckled. 'I'm not exactly a Caruso, but it was a case of any port in a storm. It's just as well that this isn't a movie with a soundtrack.'

The slides were vividly coloured, as they all had been. Jane's hair was loose and longer, and she had a scarlet hibiscus at one ear and her dress had a tight emerald green bodice with a low, square-cut neck, and a full scarlet and black skirt. She thought Broderic made a strange sound, a sort of incredulous exclamation jerked out of him, and cut off.

There was a lot of dancing and swirling skirts ... movies would have done more justice to it, but it had certainly been some show. The men were in loose white shirts and longs. Jane called over her shoulder, 'Here's one to make you really jealous, Kate—hope you won't hold it against me,' and on flashed one of Scott standing behind and to one side of Jane, his arms clasped in front of her waist. His head was bent towards her uplifted face. There was invitation in every inch of Jane, intention in every inch of Scott.

They all laughed, Kate leading the laughter, but there was a crash from the far corner. Broderic Adair's chair had gone over. Just as Giles switched on the light to see what had happened, Broderic's voice said, 'Jane! Was it only a musical? Was that *all*?'

Jane blinked against the sudden light and the tone of his voice. They faced each other over the twins' heads. The rest of the company sat glued to their chairs, save Giles, and just stared.

Jane said, with a little shake of the head, as if to clear her thoughts, 'But Broderic, I said to start with, it was a musical. What are you talking about?'

He seemed to have clean forgotten the audience. His eyes met hers, demanding truth. 'Then it wasn't you that Scott— I mean, you and Scott didn't—Jane, I can't very well explain in front of all these people ...'

She said simply, because the meaning of it all was breaking like a light over her, 'You mean—you must mean—you thought it was *me* Vanda concocted her lies about. Did you, Broderic? But how *could* you think that?'

He made a helpless gesture, as one who deplores having to do this in public. 'Well, here it comes. When you told me after Scott's first visit that you simply didn't believe he had dangled after any other girl, I came to the conclusion Vanda had lied, so when you went to Oamaru, I flew up to see her. Yes, Kate, I did.

'I trounced her for making mischief, and told her I was sure she'd made it all up. She got flaming mad and said if I didn't believe her I'd be apologising the next moment, because the camera can't lie ... and she produced a coloured photo almost identical with that last slide, Jane. If anything it was even more loving. Oh, why the devil hadn't you worn a grass skirt or something, then I might have tumbled to it? I apologised to her all right. I shall ring her up tomorrow and blister her eardrums!'

'Oh no, you won't,' said Scott. 'That's going to be *my*

privilege. When I think of the hell Kate and I have gone through, it would only be safe to do it by phone. Never mind, Kate took my word for it even before this proof, and that means everything to me.'

Jane wasn't registering much of this. She had her eyes fixed on Broderic Adair. 'Broderic, tell me. Was that why you wrote me that letter telling me I wasn't to come back here?'

'Why else? I thought you the most despicable deceiver I'd ever met, and I just wouldn't take the chance of you and Kate meeting. It was only later, when I knocked myself out and Kate arrived before I recovered consciousness, and she obviously hadn't recognised you, that I realised she must never have seen the photo. Why on earth didn't Vanda show it to you, Kate?'

Kate shrugged. 'You know my stiff-necked pride. Vanda said "I can even show you proof if you don't believe me," and I wouldn't look at it.' She giggled. 'Just as well. Jane, had I recognised you I'd have been back in the North Island in two twos, and this snarl would never have been sorted out.'

Anna Doig said, 'Well, the course of true love certainly doesn't seem to run smoothly. There are some prime examples of that right here in this room. Me? I took Calum for a drunken driver in the first hour we met. Giles swore at Lucinda for scattering his herd, Kate's love-life has been sabotaged by a false friend and now it seems as if ... ?' She put her streaky gold head on one side and regarded Jane and Broderic saucily and meaningfully.

Jane looked hastily away from her and encountered her mother's gaze, full to the brim with laughter and expectancy.

'I wish,' said Louise clearly, 'someone would tell me what this is all about!'

Jane said hastily, 'Anna just means that she and Calum had a stormy courtship, and so did Lucinda and Giles, and

Kate and Scott had a misunderstanding. That's all. Nothing more.'

'Oh yes, there is,' said Broderic Torquil Adair, 'there's lots more. Jane Esmeralda Grey, it's a bit public, I know, but you know as well as I do that if it hadn't been for this hideous mistake, I'd have proposed to you long ago. Don't you dare shut up my future twin sisters-in-law like that!'

Jane said, 'I'll never forgive you for this, Broderic Adair! After all, a girl likes to be asked, not taken for granted.'

Suddenly they were all helpless with laughter, save Jane.

Her mother said, sobering up, 'I never, in my wildest dreams, ever thought I'd be present when my daughter was proposed to.'

'I haven't accepted him yet,' said Jane in a mutter.

Broderic's hazel eyes were alight with laughter. 'Doesn't much matter, my Jane, you'll come to it. Jane, here it comes, loud and clear, will you marry me?'

'You bet I will,' said Jane unromantically and shamelessly.

There were an awful lot of bodies between him and Jane. Broderic's eyes dropped to the twins. 'What do you know? We've actually knocked them speechless. I didn't think it could be done.'

Giles Logie got to his feet from the chair he'd dropped into again. 'I don't know about you folk, but I feel decidedly *de trop*. I think this is where we should all murmur graceful farewells and fade into the darkness of the night.'

There was a protesting cry from Willy. 'You can't do that, I've got a lovely spread set out in the conservatory. And we're going to have company.'

'Company?' groaned Broderic. 'And what do you call this?' He surveyed them, grinning. 'It's more company than I want at this moment, I can tell you!'

The twins came to life. 'The carol-singers,' they said, 'from the church. They told us on Sunday they'd be here at ten-thirty, and Mother offered to put on supper for them. It was to be a surprise. When you said we were having visitors from Drumlogie, Jane, Mum made that the excuse to put all those goodies out. Come and see.'

They all trooped out to switch the lights on in the conservatory. The twins had done all the decorating. In and out of Esmeralda's hanging baskets and Rory's pulleys they had twined silver festoons. They'd brought in larch and fir-branches and had lavishly scattered glittering imitation snow on them. Rory had bought twin dolls for the top of the Christmas tree, and stars sparkled from all its twigs.

Jane felt tears prick her eyelids as she saw the photograph of Esmeralda standing under her clematis arch in pride of place on the centre table. Scott must have given it to them.

Suddenly they heard it, the first faint carolling, and they plunged the conservatory into darkness save for the lights on the tree. Presently they saw dozens of hurricane lanterns coming up through the pine-wood, and voices young and old singing on the summer air, 'O little town of Bethlehem, how still we see thee lie ...'

Jane felt an arm about her, turned her cheek to feel Broderic's cheek against her own, and said, 'Oh, Rory, what a time to pick!'

He laughed. 'Don't the sages always ask: "What is time?" and say all time is relative? For us tonight doesn't end till we've ironed it all out, even if it may be the early hours of tomorrow morning. And we've all our tomorrows ahead of us, shared tomorrows. We're going to find true solitude in which to pledge ourselves to each other.' He dropped a light kiss upon her hair just as the carol-singers reached the steps and the men got the lights on again. A merry hour followed.

The last goodbyes were said, the last sound of departing cars died down the road towards the lake ... the twins tumbled into bed. The men were in their quarters. Scott and Kate had gone up to Starlight. Scott would sleep in the guestroom there tonight. Willy looked at them smilingly and said her goodnight too.

Broderic and Jane found themselves outside in Esmeralda's hillside garden . . . and alone.

He said, looking down on her, 'Where is it to be, Jane?'

She said, 'Through the roses to the Bruach and the Adair Water. Some other night we can renew our memories on the haunch of Cruachan. Tonight I can't wait.'

He laughed. 'I can hardly recognise you in so compliant a mood.'

They walked over the rock flagstones thinking of Esmeralda. Their way took them between borders of catmint and cinnamon pinks, lavender and saxifrage. He said as they went, hand-in-hand, 'I was in such a turmoil, loving you so, distrusting you at first because you had Henry Grey's blood in you, but admiring your grit and your get-up-and-go, the way you shouldered your responsibilities.

'I found out you were all I'd ever wanted any woman to be, and I was ready to ask you to be my wife. Then Scott came in, and for the first time in my life, I knew jealousy. I saw you up on the ridge. You were holding hands. I told myself not to be stupid, but then the crunch came. I flew up to Palmerston, to save my sister's romance as I thought, and was faced with what I thought must be indisputable evidence of your perfidy. I got very bitter; I thought I must be as gullible as Kate, and that my first instincts had been right . . . not to trust a Grey. I was glad Esmeralda had gone before I found you out. I lived with my disillusionment night and day, and told myself you weren't worth grieving for, but I couldn't stop myself. I tried to do all I could to keep you away from Starlight and Kate. I couldn't trust myself not to weaken if you took up your abode here.' He stopped, then said, and his voice held a regret that tore at Jane, 'I'll never forgive myself for the anguish I caused you, and you innocent of everything . . . just a slip of a girl battling against great odds.'

'And yet,' said Jane, her voice very soft, very loving, 'you even offered that girl you despised thousands of dollars for a property she didn't own. Because in spite of everything you felt sorry for the plight in which she found herself.'

They came to a sudden stop beside a willow-sweet spot where the Adair Water widened into a pool before plunging down the brae. Broderic seized her. 'You know? You know, Jane?' Then, 'When did you find out?'

'On this day of truth, about four hours ago. Giles let it out. I was just recovering from the shock when you came to the studio in search of us. My mind was in a whirl. I couldn't imagine why you'd done it.'

He turned her round against a giant weeping willow. The moonlight then fell directly on her. He said softly, 'Green tree, green-eyed girl in a green dress ... a bewitching combination, and she asks why I did it! Oh, Jane Esmeralda, because I loved you, of course; loved you without rhyme or reason first, love you now because of what you are, honest, trustworthy, dependable. Darling, I'll make over Wedgwood House to Willy. She must never feel dependent upon the bounty of a son-in-law. We'll blast our way through the Giant's Causeway on the Stumbling-Block. I don't think I could ever have razed the old school down, with its painted green-and-white doors and its conservatory and all its memories of Esmeralda. I just kidded myself I was tough enough to do it. Jane, will you create just such a garden for us, up at Starlight? And soon, Jane, soon?'

Up the hill a sheep coughed. One bleated. Broderic's sheep. A bird twittered sleepily. Jane looked up trustingly, saw her eyes mirrored in his eyes, put up her two hands and brought his face down to hers. 'It can't be too soon for me, Broderic Torquil Adair,' she said, smiling. And thereafter found speech impossible.

The Adair Water went singing on its way.

In every issue...

Here's what you'll find:

 a complete, full-length romantic novel...illustrated in color.

 exotic travel feature...an adventurous visit to a romantic faraway corner of the world.

 delightful recipes from around the world...to bring delectable new ideas to your table.

 reader's page...your chance to exchange news and views with other Harlequin readers.

 other features on a wide variety of interesting subjects.

Start enjoying your own copies of Harlequin magazine immediately by completing the subscription reservation form.

Not sold in stores!